"That was incredible," Faith murmured

With Faith nestled against his chest, sated after hours of delicious lovemaking, Lex knew what he had to do. This was the moment. He lifted her head, making her look into his eyes. "I need you to remember something. It's very important, okay?"

"Sure," she said, obviously perplexed.

"I am in love with you."

A smile curved her mouth. "I—"

"I've been in love with you since the first moment I saw you," he continued, his voice intense. It was vitally important that she understand him. "I think you are the most remarkable woman I've ever met. I look at you and I—" He looked away, trying to find the right words. "I look at you and I melt. Something happens to me in here." He thumped his chest. "I need you to know it. I need you to remember it."

Her eyes seemed to mist over and she kissed his cheek. And then she said the words he'd been dreading. "Oh, Nash. I love you, too."

Dear Reader,

My writing career has finally come full circle. Many, many years ago I submitted my first ever romance novel to Harlequin Temptation—it was called *The Lover's Candle* and I'm eternally thankful that it never saw publication. Like me, many authors have books in their past that hold the Worst Book In The History of the World award and we happily use those manuscript pages for rough drafts and doodle paper for the kids. *Unforgettable*, though, is a book that I'm very proud of.

What happens when an author gets amnesia, then wakes up as the heroine in her wildly popular romantic-suspense books? Chaos of the first order. Especially when she first sets eyes on hunky lodge owner Lex Ellenberg and decides *he's* her hero. Only, little does she realize that Lex is about to show her what being a *real* hero is all about....

I hope you will enjoy Faith and Lex's story. I had a blast writing it. For more information on past and upcoming books, be sure to check out my Web site, www.booksbyrhondanelson.com.

Happy reading,

Rhonda Nelson

Books by Rhonda Nelson

HARLEQUIN BLAZE
 75—JUST TOYING AROUND...
 81—SHOW & TELL
115—PICTURE ME SEXY

RHONDA NELSON

UNFORGETTABLE

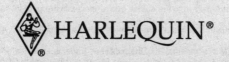

HARLEQUIN®

TORONTO • NEW YORK • LONDON
AMSTERDAM • PARIS • SYDNEY • HAMBURG
STOCKHOLM • ATHENS • TOKYO • MILAN • MADRID
PRAGUE • WARSAW • BUDAPEST • AUCKLAND

You may have tangible wealth untold;
Caskets of jewels and coffers of gold.
Richer than I you can never be—
I had a mother who read to me.
—Strickland Gillilan

This book is dedicated to my mother, Hope Whitley.
Thanks, Mom, for sharing your love of the written word,
for telling me stories and fueling my imagination.
For being a champion, a friend and confidante.
Bun love Mom.

ISBN 0-373-69173-4

UNFORGETTABLE

www.eHarlequin.com

Printed in U.S.A.

1

"WHOSE IDEA WAS THIS again?"

"Yours," Trudy said drolly.

Faith Bonner bit her bottom lip, glanced at the passing scenery as they wound their way higher and higher up into the Great Smoky Mountains of Tennessee. Despite the glorious display of fall color, a tremor of trepidation shook her tummy. "Well, it was a bad one," she said grimly.

Her assistant expelled a small breath. "No, it wasn't—it was brilliant." Smiling, she nudged Faith's shoulder. "You just need to relax. That was the purpose of coming up early, remember? I'm going to finalize all the arrangements for the *To Catch a Thief* event—which is going to be spectacular, by the way," Trudy said excitedly. "And you're going to rest."

That would be a neat trick, Faith thought, since her muscles were practically atrophied with stress. What the hell had she been thinking? Honestly, they could have hosted this publicity event in any number of fine hotels in Nashville, or any other large city, for that matter. Not in the wilds of east Tennessee, where signs like Do Not Feed Bears Under Penalty of Law were posted every several hundred feet.

While Faith appreciated nature, she nonetheless preferred her creature comforts. By all accounts, Oak Crest Lodge—their ultimate destination—had every necessary amenity, but Faith couldn't help but be a little nervous this far removed from true civilization. While she wasn't precisely a dyed-in-the-wool city girl, she still hadn't had a single camping/hiking/kayaking outdoor adventure that hadn't ended in disaster. Broken bones, snake bites, poison oak... You name it, it had most likely happened to her. She was a graceless klutz and had long ago accepted that unflattering truth about herself.

To make matters worse, she'd been attacked by a small dog as a child—a Chihuahua, for pity's sake—but the experience had been nothing short of traumatic and had left her ridiculously terrified of most animals—particularly ones with teeth. Faith's worried gaze scoured the tree line and she fidgeted in her seat. The idea that wild creatures with huge, glistening incisors roamed in these beautiful woods scared the living daylights out of her, made her stomach twist with an *oh-hell* kind of dread.

Trudy negotiated a hairpin turn. "I don't know why you're so worried about this, Faith," she chided gently. "It's not like you don't know what you're doing. Hell, you know the character—you've been writing the Zoe Wilder books for years—and you wrote the mini-mystery for this weekend. Why are you so freaked?"

Faith summoned a droll smile. "Oh, I don't know. I guess the idea of making a complete fool of myself is a little intimidating."

Trudy huffed an exasperated sigh. "You're not going to make a fool of yourself. First of all, no one but you will know if you screw up. And secondly, the fans are going to be so excited about being a part of this that nothing else will matter."

Faith had her doubts about that. She knew her readers expected her to be every bit as bold and brash, as hot and sexy as the heroine—Zoe Wilder—in her wildly popular romantic adventure books. Faith resisted the urge to snort. She and Zoe were polar opposites, couldn't be any more different. Faith had purposely given Zoe every trait she'd like to possess but, sadly, didn't.

Instead, she lived out her dreams vicariously through her audacious, chic, savvy gun-toting heroine. Through her books, *she* was beautiful, *she* was brave and fearless, charming, witty and sexy. *She* wore too-tight too-short skirts, a push-up bra and red lipstick. And, when taking care of the bad guys hadn't been enough—when Faith had found herself miserably lonely—she'd given Zoe *Nash*—a badass to end all badasses, a to-die-for heartthrob whose melting smile was so hot it could make an orchid bloom in an arctic frost.

She'd also made him the best lover in the northern hemisphere and she couldn't write a love scene between the two during which she didn't have an overwhelming orgasm. She repressed a delicate shiver.

In fact, though she'd never risk the psych ward by admitting this to anyone, Faith feared that the fictitious Nash Austin—a total figment of her imagination—had ruined her for any living male. Now how pathetic was that? She'd fallen in love with a character, a person who existed only on paper and in her mind.

Furthermore, she'd made him so damn good that no real guy could ever compare. Or at least if one did, Faith had yet to find him. If someday hell froze over and he did happen along her path, Faith knew he wouldn't be the type to be interested in her.

Men like that—or any man, for that matter—rarely gave her a second glance.

Regrettably, she seemed to blend in, like a part of the scenery.

Most of the time, Faith preferred being unremarkable. She liked order—her childhood had provided enough chaos, thank you very much—and moved through her daily routine without any glitches. She got up every morning, ran a couple of miles, came home, showered, ate breakfast, then sat down at her computer and worked on her work-in-progress until her belly rumbled. She'd eat lunch, then work until another hunger pain struck, heralding the end of that day in front of the computer.

Occasionally the routine would vary—she'd go wild and use her laptop—but for the most part, one day looked the same as another. She liked it that way. She really did. There was a strange sort of comfort in the monotony.

Until a new book came out—then things went to hell in a handbasket.

Faith had a new release every September, spent that entire month as well as the two following on tour to promote the book. She enjoyed meeting her readers, hearing their thoughts about her books, and she liked seeing new cities—but she hated the interviews and she hated when perceptive readers realized that her whole I'm-just-like-Zoe act was just that—an act. She swallowed, felt a smile tug at her lips as she watched a couple of squirrels argue over an acorn. No amount of success, no amount of money made up for those momentary feelings of inadequacy.

This year, she'd decided to offer something a little different—a *To Catch a Thief* contest—in which ten lucky fans got to spend the weekend with her and solve a mystery. Faith had run the idea past the powers that be at her publishing house, and they'd loved it. Once she'd gotten the official go-ahead, she and Trudy had designed a whodunit mystery and assigned each winner a specific character. Dossiers with instructions and a list of suspects had been sent to each guest. They would all arrive in character, ready to play.

Faith would play the part of Zoe, of course. One of the perks of being the author, she thought. Trudy was right on one score—Faith knew Zoe Wilder better than she knew herself, and to be brutally honest, she'd been equally thrilled and intimidated by the idea. A rogue wave of excitement bubbled through her, then was washed away by a monsoon of dread.

She was literally going to step into the spiked heels of her kick-ass heroine.

And if she could get over the fear of making a

complete and total fool of herself, she'd think it was cool.

"Okay," Trudy said, and from the brisk tone of her voice, she was gearing up for another verbal checklist. "Let's run over things once more, just to make sure that we're covered."

Faith suppressed a small smile. "Okay."

"Do you have a copy of the character dossiers?"

"Check."

"The winners list and accompanying information?"

"Check."

"A master copy of the mystery?"

Faith nodded. "Check."

"Your 'Zoe' wardrobe?"

"Check," Faith told her.

In fact, she'd shocked the crap out of her personal shopper at the local mall. Faith's tastes tended to lean toward soft neutrals and earth tones—her closet was a sad sea of beiges, browns and rusts. Adding Zoe's bright, slinky wardrobe had been like adding a tie-dyed T-shirt to a rack of tan turtlenecks. She'd undoubtedly look ridiculous, Faith thought—she'd gotten a wee bit carried away with sequins—but then who wouldn't? All the characters had been exaggerated, so she wouldn't be the only one who looked as if she'd just stepped out of a mental hospital.

She'd even gone by a local spy shop and picked up a few handy little gadgets, as well as a convincing-looking piece, though the only way she could defend herself with that gun would be to conk someone over the head with it.

"And John will be here Friday?"

"Right, and he's outfitted as well for his part."

Trudy chuckled. "I can't wait to see that."

"Me either," Faith replied with a reluctant smile. Her editor, John Wallace, would play the part of Nash. Faith's lips quirked. He resembled her hunky Nash about as much as she resembled Zoe, so they were even on that score. Faith heaved a small sigh.

Bears, bobcats and big scary teeth aside, she didn't doubt for a moment that the whole experience would be exciting. Though she was anxious, she still looked forward to stepping into her alter ego's shoes, at least for a little while. Of course, she would look forward to it more if she could shake this curious sense of foreboding. For reasons that escaped her, she felt...weird. Braced. Just waiting for the other shoe to drop.

Which was ridiculous, when she had Type-A

Trudy along. Faith cast her good friend and assistant a covert sidelong glance.

Trudy—while she had to be one of the most melodramatic people Faith had ever known—was profoundly efficient. Trudy wouldn't stand for any sort of chaos, any flaw, any wrinkle. She was a short, spunky dynamo in pumps, and could bark orders better than a drill sergeant when the need arose.

She was worrying needlessly, Faith decided, forcing the tension from her limbs. Everything would be fine.

"Well, I think that covers everything," Trudy finally said, having deemed them suitably prepared. "This is going to be fantastic. You'll be fantastic." Her lips curled in a knowing little grin. "You're more like Zoe than you think, you know."

Faith grunted, directed her gaze out the window. Not hardly, but she wasn't going to waste her breath arguing the point.

After what felt like several more miles up the winding mountain, past beautiful vistas and rocky meandering streams, Trudy pulled the SUV through a stacked-stone-and-cedar arch that bore the name Oak Crest Lodge. "Ah, we're here," she said needlessly.

The large A-frame stacked-stone-and-cedar

building blended in so seamlessly with the surroundings it gave the impression of sprouting from
the ground, much as the trees did. Colorful leaves
dotted the roof, lined the gutters and spilled over
the long, weather-beaten front porch. Mossy
patches and mushrooms grew along the founda-
tion, crept up through the fissures in the broken
rock.

Potted ferns and mums in varying fall shades
were planted in old washtubs, barrels and water-
ing cans, and sat in no particular order on the
porch. Grapevine wreaths graced the huge,
rounded, rough-cut cedar doors.

Faith undid her seat belt as the SUV rolled to a
stop, and quietly considered the place. A funny
feeling, not easily read, tingled in her chest, making
her shift in her seat. Beside her, Trudy rambled excitedly.

Though she'd never been here before in her life
and this lodge didn't remotely resemble her mod-
ern, two-story brick home back in trendy Brent-
wood, Faith had the strangest feeling of homecom-
ing, for lack of a better description. That same
feeling one got when seeing an old, treasured, but
seldom-seen friend.

Which was equally impossible and insane.

Though she'd led a nomadic life during her

childhood—her late parents had thought moving was a grand adventure and never stayed in one place long enough to put down roots—Faith knew they'd never traveled to this part of the state, much less stayed at this particular lodge. Honestly, Faith thought. What was wrong with her today?

Feeling ridiculous and out of sorts, she shook the feeling off, got out of the car and stretched. Her muscles had bunched in the small of her back, and her legs felt like lead.

"God, isn't this the most beautiful place you've ever seen?" Trudy enthused, her voice high-pitched with wonder. "The pictures simply didn't do it justice." She threw her head back and drew in a deep breath. "Oh, the air is so crisp and clean. This is simply fantastic."

Faith had to agree. It *was* spectacular. The overall mood of the place seemed cozy and warm. A little careworn here and there, needing a little TLC, Faith decided, eyeing the full gutters. Still, she was instantly enchanted. The place just inspired—

A flash of something big and black caught her eye, making her pause, midstretch. That cloak of foreboding she hadn't been able to shake tightened imperceptibly around her throat, and a skitter of alarm whispered over her nape, making her scalp prickle.

Faith slowly turned and in the nanosecond it took for her brain to assimilate just exactly what she was looking at—what horrifying monstrosity was barreling toward her at breakneck, slobber-spewing speed—her muscles froze with terror, locking her in place. She could barely draw a breath, much less move.

So she screamed.

Then fainted.

2

LEX ELLENBURG'S HEAD jerked up as an earsplitting scream suddenly rent the air. Oh, hell. Not Pooh again, Lex thought as a ball of dread ricocheted around his abdomen. Not Pooh, dammit. He didn't have time to deal with another lecture from the park rangers—he had too many other pressing problems to deal with.

Like keeping his fledgling lodge afloat.

He buried the ax into a log and raced to the front of the building. The young bear had been coming around a lot more lately and, while most of his guests were regulars and knew of Pooh's penchant for wandering about the lodge grounds, there was always a newbie who would see him and squeal like a wounded hog.

Then report him.

While Lex believed Pooh too tame to be a real threat to anyone, he was still a wild animal and animals could always be unpredictable. Lex snorted. Like women.

He rounded the corner and breathed a palpable

sigh of relief. Not Pooh, thank God. Only Beano. Granted, the giant black lab had pinned a small woman to the ground, but she clearly wasn't in any danger of being mauled to death. Lex's lips twisted. The worst Beano could do was drown her in doggy drool. Still, his dog knocking guests to the ground couldn't be good for business.

"Beano!" Lex bellowed sharply. "Off!"

"Off!" cried another woman, this one desperately trying to haul the giant dog off her friend. She might as well be trying to move a mountain with a spoon, for all the good it was doing. "Get off her, you great ox!" When she spied Lex, her face wilted with relief. "Thank God. Call him off. Get him *off* her!"

Tongue lolling out of the side of his mouth, Beano turned his soulful dark brown eyes toward Lex and seemed to say, *"Look what I found. A new toy."*

It was at that precise moment that Lex realized the woman on the ground seemed unnaturally still. She made no effort to shove the dog from her chest, and she wasn't screaming. Not a good sign. He mentally swore and a whole new kind of tension tightened his spine.

Pulse hammering in his ears, Lex rushed to her side, dropped to his knees, shoved the dog off her chest—"*Off, dammit!*"—and checked for any visible injuries. The worried friend crouched beside him, took the woman's hand and gently shook it. "Faith? Faith? Oh, Faith!" she cried.

No blood, thank God, Lex thought, though he was still far from relieved. He ran his hands over her limbs, checking for any broken bones, then picked up her small wrist and checked her pulse. The strong beat throbbing beneath his fingertips marginally alleviated some of the dread.

He looked up. "Did she hit her head when the dog knocked her down?"

"Faith? Oh, come on, Faith," the friend pleaded desperately, gently nudging the unconscious woman. Worry wrinkled her brow. "I don't know," she said, clearly agitated. "I was on the other side of the car. But the dog didn't knock her down. She fainted before he got to her."

Startled, Lex frowned. "Fainted?"

"She was attacked by a dog when she was a child," she said defensively, casting him an annoyed glare. She gestured irritably at Beano. "I'm sure he's probably harmless, but he charged her like a bull, for heaven's sake. That animal will have to be put up while we're here." She scowled and didn't appear to like the idea, but seemed resolved nonetheless.

Though he couldn't possibly understand what had been said, Beano whimpered, trotted over and buried his wet nose in Lex's neck.

"Go on," Lex told him, giving him an affectionate push. "I'll deal with you later," he said, exasperated. Damn dog. He didn't need this, and he didn't want to put up his dog, but under the circumstances, he didn't see where he would be left with much choice.

"Let's get her inside." He carefully lifted her in his arms and, despite the tension gathered in every muscle, couldn't help but notice that her slight frame had all the right curves, in all the right places. She felt...nice against him, soft and womanly. Her scent, something light and floral—daisies maybe?—drifted up and teased his nostrils. She had a smooth heart-shaped face, a lightly freckled button nose and a dainty chin, which would have made her simply cute...but when one factored in that full, ripe mouth, she became downright beautiful. Soft-as-silk fawn-colored curls bobbed over his arm with every step he took, and to Lex's unending astonishment, his blood simmered, igniting a pilot light in his groin.

He swallowed a bark of self-deprecating laughter. Which just went to show just how desperately he needed to get laid.

Hell, he hadn't had the time, much less the energy. Keeping the lodge in the black, practicing creative finance—which he'd become so adept at in recent months he should qualify for a damned Ph.D.—and constantly maintaining the building hadn't left him with so much as a morning to sleep in, much less time to find a woman willing to indulge in a little recreational sex.

His gaze dropped to the woman in his arms and a muscle ticked in his tense jaw. Clearly, if he had sunk to lusting over unconscious females, it was time to remedy that problem.

But there was something altogether intriguing about this particular woman, Lex thought, as his gaze inexplicably lingered on her gorgeous face far longer than it should have under the circumstances—she was unconscious, after all. It didn't stop his chest from unexpectedly tightening, nor did it account for his suddenly galloping heart. He blinked, unsettled, and forced himself to look away, to focus on getting her inside the building.

The friend hurried forward and opened the door to the lodge. Lex muttered his thanks, crossed the threshold and made his way over to one of the big leather sofas positioned in front of the fireplace. He gingerly deposited his bundle on the couch and, to his vast relief, she finally stirred. She'd been as limp as a rag doll while he'd brought her in.

The mystery woman's lids fluttered, then opened, revealing a pair of huge, heavily lashed, light brown eyes. They were the color of melted caramel, Lex thought, swallowing past a curious knot in his throat. That bizarre tourniquet around his chest tightened, pushing the butterflies in his belly farther behind his navel. He went momentarily deaf while staring into those utterly captivating eyes—couldn't hear a single sound—and the sensation left him feeling more than a little disturbed.

Her brow wrinkled and a wondering, gorgeous smile bloomed across her oh-so-sexy lips. He felt that smile clear to his toes, most particularly behind his zipper. *"Nash?"* she breathed reverently.

The friend eagerly bumped him aside. "Faith! Oh, thank God! Are you all right? Are you hurt?"

Nash? Lex wondered, bewildered. *Who the hell was Nash?*

Confusion filled Faith's eyes, lined her forehead. She gazed back and forth between them, then inhaled sharply, closed her eyes and groaned. "I— What— *Oh, God.*"

"The dog charged you," the friend explained, "but Mr.—" She shot him a questioning glance.

"Ellenburg," Lex supplied, still bewildered by his intense reaction to her.

"Mr. Ellenburg has assured me that the animal will be put up for the duration of our stay."

The look she gave him dared him to argue and, though he knew it was unreasonable, he would like nothing better than to argue. Lex didn't want to put up his dog, dammit—he'd be miserable. Furthermore, Beano was harmless and it seemed wholly unfair to punish him for the sins of another animal.

Still, he couldn't afford to lose their business— any business, for that matter, and he assumed that they were part of the Zoe Wilder festivities this weekend—and he certainly couldn't afford to displease that group. He frowned at the grim reminder. The ramifications were simply too horrible to contemplate. Lex finally jerked his head in an affirmative nod. The woman clearly had been terrified. Hell, she'd fainted, hadn't she? Knowing that, he could hardly allow the dog to run free.

"I'm truly sorry," Lex told her. "It won't happen again."

She swung her legs off the couch, sat up and gingerly massaged her temples. A leaf fell out of her hair and bits of dirt and debris clung to her beige sweater and matching pants. A pair of identical paw prints stamped her chest.

"Don't worry about it," she said wearily in a soft throaty voice that brought to mind rumpled sheets and naked limbs. Unbelievably, white-hot lust licked at Lex's veins, stirred in his loins. An adorable blush staining her cheeks, she swiped at some of the damage. "No, uh, lasting harm done."

Lex slowly released a pent-up breath. Thankfully, she seemed more embarrassed than pissed off, and that worked to his advantage. "How about we get you checked in? See if we at Oak Crest can redeem ourselves."

Seemingly relieved that all was right with...Faith, if he remembered correctly, the friend stuck out her hand. "An excellent idea. I'm Trudy Weaver, Mr. Ellenburg. We've spoken many times."

The tentative smile that had curled his lips froze as she pumped his outstretched hand. A litany of inventive, rapid-fire curses streamed through his stalled brain. His gaze darted back and forth between the two women and he experienced a moment of uncomfortable panic. If *this* was Trudy Weaver, Lex thought, then *that*—the woman she'd called Faith—must be Faith Bonner, the famous author he was counting on to help his lodge squeak through another season.

What with all the corporately owned chains popping up on his side of the mountain, Lex's mom-and-pop business had taken a beating. He didn't know how much longer he could hold on, but the idea of selling out—or giving up—simply wasn't an option. He'd already refused two very generous offers, both of which had come from an anonymous party. Regardless, Lex hadn't even been tempted. His grandfather had built this lodge. Had logged the lumber himself.

In addition, his dad had practically killed himself—he'd died of a heart attack year before last, while patching a spot on the roof—trying to maintain it. Too much Ellenburg sweat, blood and tears had gone into this place to let it go belly-up now. So long as there was breath left in his body Lex wouldn't sell. He had to make things work. Still...

Of all the guests Beano might have bowled over, it had to be her.

Oh, hell.

"Er, it's nice to finally meet you," Lex eventually managed to say. What a damn nightmare. He sucked in a slow breath and waited expectantly for an introduction to confirm his grim suspicions.

Smiling, she gestured to Faith. "This is Faith Bonner. Faith is going to take a couple of days to re-lax while you and I work out the final details of the *To Catch a Thief* event."

Lex nodded, glanced at the woman in question and offered a tongue-in-cheek smile. "Well, despite recent evidence to the contrary, Oak Crest is a great place to relax. There's something for everyone here."

Faith wore a bemused expression, continued to stare at him until the silence stretched beyond the comfortable and Lex began to wonder if maybe he had something stuck in his teeth. Those melted-caramel orbs lingered until he had to forcibly quell the urge to squirm, which he was strongly tempted to do anyway because every hair on his body stood on end when she looked at him. It was truly bizarre, this reaction he had to her. It was almost as if he knew her. As if some part of him recognized her. But that wasn't possible.

"Er..." Trudy's slightly distressed gaze bounced between them, then, thankfully, she moved to fill the odd silence. "I'm sure she'll love it here." She bustled Faith toward the reception desk. "What say we get checked in, shall we?"

Seemingly blinking out of a trance, Faith cast him a sheepish glance and her pale complexion brightened with pink color. "R-right."

Praying that no other disasters would befall them before he got them checked in and safely escorted to their rooms, Lex made quick work of the process. In short order, though Faith had continued to stare at him through the corner of her eye and not-so-covertly study him during the entire curiously stressful process, Lex finally booked the two women into a couple of his nicest rooms.

Then he went to the kitchen with the intention of downing a beer—he'd undoubtedly earned it after that bizarre episode—but swiftly substituted a soda for the alcohol after a stern look from his uncle.

George's lined face folded into a frown. "What's the problem?"

The problem? Lex thought with a silent laugh. Would that there were only one. Regrettably, he'd just added one more to a list of many, and this one was startlingly disturbing—he'd fallen instantly in lust with Faith Bonner. There could be no other explanation for his persistent hard-on, or his acute fascination with her mouth, or the overwhelming case of gooseflesh still pebbling his skin.

Nevertheless, he couldn't imagine sharing that little tidbit with his uncle, so instead he related the Beano incident. "I've put him out back," Lex told him, finishing the tale. "But I know he's going to hate it."

George rubbed his bristled chin. "Yeah, well, not as bad as you'll hate it if that fancy author and her weird fans take their business elsewhere." He nodded curtly. "Beano'll be all right. It's just for a few days."

Lex inclined his head. Leave it to George to sum it up so succinctly. His uncle had strong opinions and didn't mind sharing them whether asked or not. Lex grinned. It was part of George's charm. He was a little rough around the edges, but Oak Crest wouldn't be the same without him. Couldn't function without him, truth be told.

The minute his mother had retired to Florida—it had been too painful for her to remain at the lodge after his father died—George had set up shop in the kitchen and, in Lex's opinion, there wasn't a finer cook on this side of the mountain. He didn't know what he'd do without him and, thankfully, wouldn't ever have to find out. George was as much a part of the lodge now as the timbers that held it together.

Which was all the more reason why Lex had to keep it afloat. Too many people depended on him, George included. Lex shot a dark look at his crotch—at the hard-on that wouldn't end. Rather than worrying about gorgeous Faith Bonner with her porn-star lips, he should probably try to concentrate on keeping a roof over their heads, he thought, disgusted.

SWEET HEAVEN, Faith thought, instantly calling Lex Ellenburg's image to the forefront of her mind, *he looked just like Nash.*

Just. Like. Nash.

Her heart tripped an unsteady beat in her chest, and forcing air into her shallow lungs was proving to be damn near impossible. Her stomach somersaulted, did a few other gymnastic moves guaranteed to make her insides alternately soar and plummet. Her hands shook and her mouth grew parched.

He had the same coal-black hair and ice-blue eyes, the dimple in one lean cheek and that sexy cleft in his chin. Even the thin jagged scar that slashed across his temple. He was impossibly tall and broad shouldered, built like a Greek god, which seemed appropriate because she was more than willing to physically worship him...and certainly wouldn't mind offering herself up as a sacrifice, either.

The man had every single physical trait she'd given Nash Austin more than four years ago. It absolutely astounded her. Blew her mind.

When she'd first opened her eyes and he'd been leaning over her... Faith gave a delicate shiver. Her foolish heart had leaped with joy and every single cell in her body had sung in recognition of him.

Need had broadsided her, overwhelming and insistent, achy and hot.

And then reality had intruded in the form of her nearly weeping, overly dramatic assistant, and Faith's memory had returned full force. The dream had receded, making her feel like a complete and total moron.

Honestly, it hadn't been bad enough that she'd had to faint, make a fool of herself. No, she'd had to do it up nicely, blink drunkenly at him and whisper "Nash" like a lovesick fool. Where was a good crater when you needed one? Faith wondered, her face flushing with renewed embarrassment.

She'd taken one look at that big black dog—totally harmless, according to both Lex and Trudy—and she'd screamed and fainted like a ravished virgin in a bad B movie. One bad experience with a dog and she'd been scarred for life. Faith hated the weakness, hated the character flaw. Dogs were supposed to be man's best friend. Just because she'd had an unfortunate run-in with a bipolar Chihuahua twenty years ago shouldn't make her so damn phobic about them now.

"So what do you think of the place?" Trudy asked. "Nice, huh?"

Faith nodded, made a concerted effort to focus on her friend. Trudy had gone to a lot of trouble to make this a memorable weekend for her and her fans. The least she could do was show a little enthusiasm. "It's lovely."

Trudy had been admiring the view from the window, but turned to face her. A concerned line creased her brow and a cloud of worry darkened her hazel eyes. "Are you sure you're okay? You took quite a fall."

"Positive." Faith shot her a sheepish look. "I can't believe I fainted." She rolled her eyes, rubbed an imaginary wrinkle from between her own brows. "God, how embarrassing." She exhaled mightily, dropped onto the foot of the bed and fell back.

Trudy's eyes twinkled. She crossed her arms over her chest and rocked back lightly on her heels. "It was positively dramatic."

Faith humphed under her breath. "Great."

"Particularly the way Mr. Ellenburg raced around the building, then scooped you up in his powerful arms and brought you inside. He'd been quite worried, you know."

Faith snorted indelicately. "I imagine the word *lawsuit* was flashing through his head."

Trudy toed her shoes off and sank into one of the big cushy chairs positioned in front of the window. She hummed thoughtfully under her breath. "That was not the impression I got."

Her silly heart did a cartwheel. "Oh?"

"There was definitely something else at work there," Trudy said consideringly. "His eyes seemed magnetized to your body...as were his hands. He did a *thorough* search."

Heat flared in her belly and her head whipped around to where Trudy sat. "What?"

"Not to worry," Trudy chuckled. "He didn't molest you...but I wouldn't mind him checking *me* over for broken bones." She gave a misty sigh. "It was very romantic."

So he'd felt her up and she didn't even have the pleasure of remembering it? Faith thought, unreasonably disappointed. Well, wasn't that just par for the course? A great-looking guy had his hands all over her, swept her into his arms and carried her to safety—a truly heroic moment, probably the only one she'd ever have in her life—and she had absolutely no recall of it whatsoever.

Damn.

Trudy slid her a sly glance. "He wasn't the only one who seemed intrigued. You, for instance, couldn't keep your eyes off him."

Faith knew she should offer some token protest, but couldn't muster the effort. What was the point? Her gaze had been glued to him like flypaper, as the rest of her would have been if she'd let herself.

She'd been utterly fascinated by him. Hadn't been able to help herself. She shot her friend a slightly embarrassed look. "I know," she admitted. "But doesn't he remind you of someone?"

Surely she wasn't the only one who saw it, Faith thought. The resemblance was so strong that anyone who was familiar with her work should be able to spot it. Trudy most definitely should.

Her friend seemed to consider the question for a moment, then to Faith's astonishment, she shook her head. "No, I can't say that he does."

"Think, Trudy," Faith pressed, rolling over onto her side. "Black hair, blue eyes, scar at the temple. Sound familiar?"

Trudy gave her a blank look. "Should it?"

Annoyed, she sat up. Good grief. Trudy critiqued for her, proofread. How could she not know? "Yes," Faith said, thoroughly exasperated.

Trudy offered a small shrug. "Sorry, honey. I'm lost."

If she wasn't reading her books any closer than that, she might be fired, Faith thought ominously. "Trudy," she said with exaggerated patience. "He looks like *Nash*."

Trudy's perplexed expression was not comforting. "Nash?"

"Yes, Nash."

She gave her head a small shake. "No, he doesn't."

"Yes, he does," Faith insisted. "Black hair, blue eyes, and the scar. He's tall, dark and handsome. He's Nash," she insisted.

"Well, he's not how I pictured Nash," Trudy said skeptically. "Not how I pictured him at all."

Faith blinked. "He's not?"

"No." She chuckled under her breath, cocked her head and assessed her with an annoyingly shrewd gleam that made Faith want to alternately scream and squirm. "But it's funny that you think he does, isn't it?"

Funny? Faith thought. No, it was many things...but funny wasn't one of them. Disconcerting, unsettling, angst-inspiring, a wee bit thrilling and possibly disastrous. But funny?

Nuh-uh.

3

"IS THERE ANYTHING ELSE?" Lex asked. He couldn't imagine that being possible—Trudy Weaver had thought of absolutely everything and he couldn't imagine that a single detail had escaped the woman's attention—but he felt obliged to ask the question, anyway.

She smiled, efficiently powered off her PDA and slipped it into her bag. "No, I think that's got it. We're really looking forward to this weekend. To my knowledge, none of the popular romantic adventure fiction writers have ever planned a weekend quite like this one. We really want it to be a success. If it is, this could turn into a yearly thing for us."

That would be nice, Lex thought, particularly if they continued to use his lodge. This had simply been a bad year. Several high-dollar repairs had been necessary. His central heat and A/C unit—a relatively new one, at that—had unexpectedly gone out, his computer system had fritzed, and for reasons he and his exterminator had never been able to discern, he'd been suddenly overrun with cockroaches back in the spring. Huge ones, some not even native to this area, and it had cost a small fortune in fees to get rid of the nasty creatures.

But things were looking up, Lex decided. His flat-lined spirits experienced a promising arc. "I'm sure everything will run smoothly. You can rest assured that my staff and I will do our part to see that it does."

Smiling, she stood. "I'm counting on it."

Lex moved to his feet as well and felt compelled to clear the air one more time about the Beano incident. He shoved a hand through his hair. "I wanted to apologize again about the dog. I've put him up. Is, er...Mrs. Bonner all right?" he asked, unintentionally putting a subtle emphasis on the Mrs. part.

Now what in the hell had made him fish for that tidbit? Lex wondered, thoroughly annoyed. He presently had too many things to concern himself with to be wondering whether or not a certain gorgeous author was married or not. More things to worry about than that sexy mouth, or those soft fawn curls, or those warm brown eyes. Another snake of heat coiled in his belly at the thought, forcing him to expel a slow breath.

Trudy paused, gave him a lingering, enigmatic

look that made the tops of his ears burn. Her lips
slid into a small smile. "It's *Ms.* Bonner, and yes,
she's fine."

Feeling ridiculous, he nodded awkwardly.
"Good."

She gave him another curiously probing look,
traced his features with her gaze, then mumbled
under her breath, "Nope, I just don't see it."

Lex blinked. "I'm sorry?"

"Nothing," she said smoothly. "Do you read the
Zoe Wilder novels, Mr. Ellenburg?"

"I haven't yet," Lex admitted, embarrassed. It
had been on his to-do list, but for various reasons,
that particular item kept getting shuffled to the bottom of the page. There was always something that
needed to be done—some task left unfinished—
and reading was simply a luxury he hadn't had
time for of late.

"Oh, you should," she admonished, clearly scan-
dalized. "Faith is phenomenally talented. Her
characters—Zoe Wilder and Nash Austin—are
larger than life, very vivid." She heaved a small
sigh. "No one writes action adventure quite like
her. She's the best. And this newest book...it's the
best one yet."

He crossed his arms over his chest. "Oh, really?"

"Yes." She shifted a bit closer, as though sharing

an important secret. "The cliff-hanger at the end of book three—*Death By Design*—is revealed on the very first page of the prologue and it just gets better and better from there. It's my new favorite." She chuckled, rocked back on her heels. "Actually, *every* new book is my new favorite," she confided.

Lex laughed as well. She was clearly very passionate about her boss's work. "I'll be sure and check them out. I just haven't had the time."

"Oh, make the time," Trudy insisted. "You won't regret it."

Lex scratched his temple. "So are you playing a part this weekend, or are you just supervising behind the scenes?" Though it didn't sound like anything he would particularly enjoy, Lex couldn't help but be a little curious about the idea.

She sighed wistfully. "I'm supervising behind the scenes. Faith wanted to me to play the part of Zoe." She lowered her voice. "She's very anxious about it, but the fans expect her to do it, and she mustn't let them down. After all, that's the whole purpose of this weekend. She wrote it, the mystery, that is, so she should be all right."

Now that was interesting, Lex thought, intrigued. He arched a brow. "Why doesn't she want to do it?"

Trudy winced regretfully. "She doesn't feel comfortable. You'd have to read the books to fully understand. Faith is worried that she won't be able to pull off playing Zoe. Zoe is one tough cookie," she conceded with a thoughtful nod. "She's a kick-butt heroine. Brash, brave and sexy, wears slinky clothes and red lipstick. Nothing like Faith. Faith's on the shy side, likes things calm and orderly. Sedate." Trudy chuckled. "Zoe is far from sedate. Still," she sighed, "I think that Faith is a whole lot more like Zoe than she realizes, and playing the part this weekend, I hope, will go a long way toward showing her that."

Another intriguing item, Lex thought, as though he needed to know another. Hell, he'd been instantly enchanted with her. Probably the less he knew about her, the better, but to his immense consternation and stupidity, that didn't keep him from fishing for more. "And this Nash Austin character," Lex said. "He's her hero?"

Trudy bobbed her head in assent. "Right. Her editor, John Wallace, is going to play his part. Faith said she couldn't do it with a stranger, that it would simply be too difficult, too embarrassing." Trudy's eyes twinkled again and she regarded him closely. "The characters have a very steamy relationship." She bounced on the balls of her feet. "They positively burn up the pages."

A sickening sensation swelled in his stomach, preventing him from making a comment. He grunted noncommittally and forced his lips into what he hoped resembled a smile. Time to cut bait, Lex decided abruptly. "Well, if everything is settled," he told her, "I have a few things I need to attend to."

Like splitting wood for tonight's fire. Regrettably, there was no wood fairy who would take care of the job for him, and he couldn't afford to buy it by the cord, a luxury his competitors enjoyed. Like most everything else around here, he had to take care of it himself. He kept a minimal, yet well-trained staff, and had promised Christmas bonuses to them for taking on additional duties not found in their typical job descriptions. Thanks to Faith Bonner and her group, Lex would have enough money to make good on that promise as well as take care of a few pressing renovations—ones that were shuffled to the end of the list while he'd been fixing everything else that had gone kaput this season.

"Oh, certainly," she told him. "I think we've covered everything."

"Good. I'll see you in the dining room this evening, then?"

"We'll be there." With that, Trudy took her leave.

Lex waited until she was out of earshot before he expelled a relieved breath. He didn't have a problem discussing menu changes, or various decorations, or helping add little clues for the upcoming event.

He did, however, have a problem thinking about Faith Bonner and her editor recreating scenes from her books in which they "burned up the pages." For reasons he didn't care to explore, the idea made him feel as if he'd eaten bad shrimp. Made him want to put his fist through a wall. Made him want to haul her to his bedroom and burn up the sheets, an act he'd make certain she'd find more agreeable than any flesh session she might dream up for her books.

Which was completely out of the question.

Time to eliminate thought with action, Lex decided abruptly. He stopped by the front desk and told George where to find him if something came up, then headed toward the back.

The moment he stepped out into the porch, Beano lumbered to his feet and issued a short impatient howl, which meant one thing—*please let me out of here.* He'd gotten too big for that pen, Lex thought absently, regretting again having to put him up. He winced. "Sorry, buddy. Maybe later."

His skin suddenly prickled and he knew before

he heard the creak of the rocker she was there. His step momentarily faltered. "Hi," he managed to murmur. "Enjoying the view?"

She toed the rocker to a stop. "Yes, I am. It's gorgeous. So much color," she said with a sigh. "It's truly beautiful."

That weird connection he'd noted before made his scalp tingle, and simply looking at her caused a curious knot of anticipation to form in his belly. Lex told his feet to keep moving, to descend the steps and move toward the woodpile, so it was quite disconcerting when they led him across the porch, where he leaned against the railing right in front of her.

"Every year I think that we'll never have a prettier fall, and then the leaves start to change and inevitably prove me wrong." He sighed as his gaze drifted proudly over the rugged terrain of his mountain. "I think it's the landscape on this side of the mountain that makes the difference. All those valleys and ravines."

She nodded thoughtfully, gestured toward the black Lab and winced. Tension vibrated off her slim frame and it occurred to him that she probably wouldn't have ventured outside to enjoy the view if Beano hadn't been penned. "I'm really sorry about your dog," she said. "He's miserable, isn't he?"

"Ah, he'll be all right," Lex told her, watching the breeze flirt with her long curls. His gaze drifted to her lips and unwanted awareness sizzled along his nerve endings. "I'll let him come in with me tonight and all will be forgiven." He'd have to, otherwise other animals might mistake his dog for bait. He was a sitting duck in that pen. "I'm just sorry that he frightened you. Trudy mentioned you'd been attacked by a dog before."

"When I was little," she confirmed with a nod. "Still, it was no reason to faint." She shot him an embarrassed look. "Thanks for, uh, taking care of me, bringing me in and all that."

"No thanks necessary. I just wish he hadn't frightened you." Lex blew out a breath. "He's big, but he's harmless. He doesn't realize his own strength."

She gazed dubiously at Beano down in the pen and looked as though she'd like nothing better than to believe him. Still, he could read the fear in every line of her body, from the faintly worried line between her brows to the rigid way she sat in the chair.

Lex grimaced. "What kind of dog attacked you?" Probably a chow. Those animals had a reputation for attacking, particularly children. They were intimidated by humans who were larger than them, which put smaller adults and children at risk.

She rolled her eyes and a smile teased her lips. "I'm too embarrassed to say."

Hmm. Not a chow then, or any of the larger breeds, obviously, or she wouldn't be embarrassed. His lips twisted into a grin. "Was it a poodle?"

That melted-caramel gaze cut in his direction. "Worse."

Worse? What could be worse than a poodle? What could be more ignoble than being attacked by a poodle? "Oh?"

She heaved a resigned sigh. "It was a Chihuahua."

A shocked chuckle burst from his lips before he managed to swallow the rest of it. It took a tremendous amount of effort to flatten his lips. "A Chihuahua?"

She cast him a droll look. "Yes, a mentally unstable Chihuahua. He was in the throes of an identity crisis at the time."

Lex crossed his arms over his chest, the woodpile and all the other pressing things on his to-do list forgotten. "An identity crisis, eh? How so?"

"He thought he was a rottweiler."

She delivered the line deadpan and this time he didn't even attempt not to laugh, but let the sound rumble up from deep in his chest.

"Go ahead and laugh," she teased indignantly, chuckling herself now. She pushed her sweater sleeves up and showed him her forearms. Tiny bite scars slashed over her skin. "It was very traumatic to a little kid. He wasn't all that small to a six-year-old, and teeth are teeth. That damn dog scared the hell out of me."

Lex's laughter tittered to a halt. She was right, of course. It would have been very frightening to a child. Still, when one thought about being attacked by a vicious dog, a Chihuahua was hardly the first breed that leaped to mind.

"I'm sorry," he told her, making a concerted effort to wipe the lingering smile from his lips. "I shouldn't have laughed."

"Oh, hell," she sighed. She pulled her sleeves back down. "It's all right. It *is* funny. I know it is. I just wish that I could get past this fear of dogs. No matter how I try to reason it away, laugh it away, the fear is still there. It's more annoying than anything else and I *hate* the weakness."

Lex inclined his head. "You have every reason to be afraid. Regardless of how big or little the dog might have been, it still attacked you. There is nothing to be ashamed of."

"I'm more embarrassed than ashamed." She gestured toward the dog. A note of irritation entered her voice. "And now your poor dog, poor—" She scowled adorably. "What's your dog's name?"

"Beano."

"Poor Be—" She paused at the beginning of what sounded like a grand soliloquy of self-disgust and comically quirked a brow. "Beano?"

He flattened his lips. "Yes, Beano."

"Er...why did you name your dog after an anti-gas product?"

Lex smiled. "Spend a little time around him, and believe me, you'll understand the significance."

A slow grin worked its way across those unbelievably sexy lips, and her light brown eyes sparkled with humor. "Do I really want to?"

Lex gave his head a small shake, rubbed the back of his neck. "Probably not."

Her gaze drifted anxiously to the dog again and Lex followed her line of sight. Beano had lain down once more and pressed his nose against the chain link fence in a display of abject doggy misery. His brows alternately lifted and settled as he looked back and forth at them.

"You're absolutely certain he won't bite?" she asked, worrying her bottom lip.

"I'm certain," Lex said confidently. "He's never bitten anyone. Oh, he might jump up on you, give you a muddy, slobbery hug, but he won't bite."

She nodded once. "Then don't leave him penned up. It's not fair."

Lex quirked a brow. "You're sure?"

"I'm sure."

"And you won't faint again?"

"Let's hope not," she said grimly. "If you don't mind, though, wait until I go in. I've got a couple of things I need to get out of the car."

"Sure. Would you like me to get them for you?" Lex offered. The last thing he needed to do was look for a reason to spend any more time with her, but he couldn't seem to help himself. He wanted to be with her, felt *compelled* to be with her.

She shook her head. "Nah, it's just a couple of little things. My laptop and the book I was reading, but thanks for asking."

"No problem."

To Lex's unreasonable disappointment, she stood. "Well, I'm going to head around that way." She glanced at the dog again, chewed the side of her bottom lip. "Why don't you give me five minutes before you let him out?"

Lex chuckled softly. "Sure." A thought struck him and before he could issue the order to his brain not to speak, his mouth formed the words. "Listen, would you like me to help you get over your fear of dogs? Beano would be the perfect animal for the job."

She paused and an equally hopeful yet dubious expression claimed her features. "You could do that?"

Lex gave a hesitant nod. "I think so."

She seemed to mull it over. "It would definitely help me out, particularly for this weekend. Zoe isn't going to look like the badass she's supposed to be if she's afraid of a friendly dog." She arched a brow. "I'm assuming Trudy covered all the particulars about the *To Catch a Thief* event?"

"She did. Sounds like a lot of fun," he lied. Sounded like a lot of trouble, nothing he'd ever enjoy doing, at any rate. On the rare occasions Lex had any free time, he preferred to spend it rafting on the creek, or fishing. Not playing pretend with a bunch of amateur sleuths. Still, to each his own, he supposed.

"I'm playing Zoe—who is completely fearless—and I'm going to look like an idiot if I faint because of the dog." She paused consideringly. "If you could help me out with him, I would really appreciate it."

"I would be happy to," Lex told her, ridiculously pleased. "Why don't we start after dinner?" That would give him time to take care of everything around here, shower and shave.

She nodded. "Sure."

"Great. I'll see you then." Lex followed Faith as she descended the steps. An awkward pause ensued when they reached the bottom. He could feel a goofy grin on his lips and couldn't seem to tear his gaze away from hers. She was studying him intently again, making him feel as if she'd put his face under a microscope. Pride demanded that he be flattered, but he couldn't help feeling a little bewildered as well, a sensation he'd been experiencing quite a bit since she got here.

"Er...is something wrong?" Lex finally asked.

She started, inhaling sharply, and her cheeks turned rosy with embarrassment. "No, nothing is wrong. Forgive me for staring. It's just you, uh, bear a remarkable resemblance to someone I know." She laughed self-consciously, crossed her arms over her chest. "Sorry."

Probably someone she knew intimately, Lex thought, given the way her creamy cheeks had bloomed with color. He pulled in a tight breath through his nostrils and fought an irrational wave of jealously.

Her brow furrowed with perplexity. "Would you mind if I asked you a personal question, Mr. Ellenburg?"

"Not at all, and call me Lex."

"Okay...Lex. How did you get that scar on your temple?"

Was that what she'd been staring at? Honestly, it was a small scar, hardly disfiguring. He'd even been told that it added character to his face. He shifted, suddenly ill at ease. "Well, I wish I could say that I got it during the Gulf War, or something equally heroic."

"But you didn't?"

He grinned, passed a hand over his face. "No...it was a bike accident. The chain broke at an inopportune moment. I landed in a blackberry bush and came out a little worse for the wear."

Eyes glittering with undisguised laughter, she inclined her head. "Oh, I see."

"The mission was heroic, though. At the time I was pretending to be a superhero." He rocked back on his heels. "I flew, too. Right over the handle bars."

She chuckled. "Ouch."

"Ouch was right." Lex shook his head, lost in the

memory. "My mother picked briars out of my hide for days."

"I'll bet." Faith glanced at the dog again, who'd begun to pace his cage. "Don't forget to give me five minutes," she reminded Lex, taking a couple of steps backward.

"I won't." Still laughing softly under his breath, he watched Faith walk away. She moved gracefully and the swing of her hips was positively mesmerizing. In addition to being one of the sexiest women he'd ever seen, she had an ass that simply would not quit. Full and heart-shaped, set off by a small, barely there waist. Perfect. Need pumped through his veins, making his blood and reflexes sluggish, which would explain why he hadn't moved an inch, hadn't continued to the woodpile that awaited his attention.

He admonished the dog to be patient—Beano had reared up on his hind legs and pawed agitatedly at the cage—then, cursing himself, Lex bustled into action. He had absolutely no business looking at her like that, much less thinking about how damn sexy she was. He didn't have time for romance, dammit. He had to keep the lodge afloat. End of story.

Was he intrigued by her? Yes.

Was she hot? Most definitely.

But she was off-limits.

Lex set a piece of wood up on the chopping block and swung the ax with a little more force than was necessary to cleave the piece. Beano whimpered in his cage.

The realization was more depressing than it should have been under the circumstances. Hell, they'd just met.

Still, there was something about Faith Bonner that made him want to watch her, made him want to listen to the sound of her voice, made him want to kiss those carnal lips and see if they were as soft and talented as they looked. If he'd ever been this instantly intrigued and attracted to a woman, it had been so long ago he couldn't recall it.

Lex exhaled mightily. But in the end, it simply didn't matter. She was a guest—the guest that ultimately assured his season—and he simply couldn't afford to let his baser needs get the better of him. The head with the brain had to maintain control. Too much rode on the outcome.

A low growl suddenly issued from Beano's throat, then for the second time in one day he heard a woman's earsplitting scream.

Faith.

Beano barked **madly** in his cage, sending Lex's heart rate into **overdrive**. If Beano was in his cage, then something else had frightened her. Something—

Oh, hell.

Ax in hand, Lex raced around to the front of the lodge again. He looked first to Faith—who appeared to have fainted again—then to the hindquarters of a lumbering bear cutting a path away from the lodge.

Lex swore hotly, dropped the ax and hurried to her side, his intestines turning to lead. Fear made his heart threaten to explode from his chest, made his knees weak. Blood oozed from her temple and she was as pale as a piece of parchment.

"Faith?" he called, gently gathering her into his arms again. "Faith? Can you hear me?"

A small groan escaped her lips and her eyes fluttered open once more. She frowned when she saw him. Déjà vu, Lex thought, limp with relief.

"Dammit, Nash," she groaned irritably. "My head hurts. What the hell happened?"

Profoundly relieved, he felt a laugh stutter out of his mouth. Nash again, eh? "Come on. I'll take you inside."

She twisted in his arms, tried to look over his shoulder. "Did that bastard Boyle get the jump on me?" she asked heatedly. "Please tell me he didn't."

Boyle? Who the hell was Boyle? "No one got the jump on you. You fainted again."

Her eyes flashed with outrage and she tried to wriggle out of his arms. "I have never fainted in my life, Nash, as you well know." She glowered at him. "What are you playing at?"

An alarm sounded in Lex's head and he paused to consider her. Something wasn't right here. He didn't know precisely what, but knew it all the same. She was acting...weird. "I'm not playing at anything. I think you may have seen Pooh," he said grimly.

"Pooh who?" she asked, clearly bewildered. "Is that some sort of code name I'm not familiar with?" She growled under her breath. "If Larson has left me out of another key briefing, heads are gonna roll. I mean it, Nash. I'm sick of his commando tactics."

Larson? Briefing? Commando tactics? Lex's head whirled with confusion. What the hell?

"Darling, you know how I love it when you carry me around—" she nuzzled his ear and her voice lowered to a suggestive purr "—but unless you're planning on carrying me to bed, I wish you'd put me down."

The warning bell he'd heard seconds ago became a full-throttle alarm. A finger of trepidation slid down his spine. Frowning, Lex lowered her to her feet and steadied her when she would have swayed. She looped her arms around his neck and brushed those carnal lips he'd just been fantasizing about over his mouth. Heat detonated in his loins, pushed his rod immediately to attention.

He drew back. "Faith, I'm not—"

She scowled. "Faith? Darling, you know I prefer that you use my own name when we're alone."

"Your own name?" he asked skeptically. That bad-shrimp sensation returned full force.

"Yes," she said, clearly exasperated with him. "My own name—*Zoe*."

The bottom dropped out of his stomach.

"It keeps me grounded, particularly when we're on a mission. I'm Faith and Candy, Lisa and Monica and all those other names when I'm with other people." Her intense gaze searched his. "You're the only person I can be Zoe with. Please remember that, okay? It's a little thing, but it's important to me." She smiled then, and laced her fingers through his. "Now, come along, Nash. We have a jewel thief to catch, remember?"

Oh, sweet Lord, Lex thought, his mind racing. What in God's name had just happened? What the hell was going on? What—

She suddenly jerked him forward, ensuring that he'd find out...whether he wanted to or not.

4

"IT'S TEMPORARY TRAUMATIC amnesia, brought about by the blow to the head," Doc Givens explained. He mopped a hand over his face. "I've heard about it before, of course, but this is the first time I've ever seen it happen."

Lex absorbed the impact of the doctor's words as he and Trudy stood out in the hall of the small office, while Faith dressed after her examination. She'd balked at coming to the doctor's office, calling the cut on her temple the "merest scratch," but he and Trudy had both insisted. He had to give Trudy credit, she'd recovered well from the initial shock of learning that her boss and friend suddenly believed that she was the heroine of her own books.

Lex'd had to explain what had happened—while repeatedly reassuring an irritated "Zoe" that Boyle hadn't gotten the drop on her—to Trudy, who, though bewildered and worried, nonetheless smoothly segued into one of Faith's characters—Melanie, an assistant.

Trudy's brow knitted in annoyed perplexity.

"But I've researched traumatic amnesia before for Faith and the kind of amnesia you're talking about would take a more serious blow to the head, one that would likely cause brain damage." She fidgeted irritably. "This doesn't make any sense."

"Normally, I would agree," the doctor told her, "but remember the brain is a mysterious organ. Medical research has made many strides in learning how it functions, but there is still more unknown than known. This is her heroine, a woman she knows as well as herself—a woman who likely is based somewhat on herself—or, more likely, who she wants to be. It was the last thing she'd written, correct?"

Trudy nodded. "Yes. She won't start the next book until promotion for this one is finished."

"Then it's fresh on her mind. It's what 'Zoe' would be doing. She's been preparing for the role, had even gotten the wardrobe, you say. For all we know, the blow to the head may have been all her subconscious needed to catapult her into the fantasy."

Equally astounded and numb, Lex blew out a breath. "So she believes she's at my lodge to catch a thief?"

"That would be my guess, yes," Doc replied.

Of all the things that had gone wrong this year,

this simply had to be the kicker. He was astounded. Utterly astounded. "So what do we do now? Do we play along? Or do we try to tell her who she is, jog her memory?"

Doc looked up quickly. "You shouldn't do anything of the sort. I'm afraid you'll have to play along. To do anything else might send her deeper into this fantasy. When she's ready to come back, she will."

Lex swallowed the urge to curse. "How long do you think that will take?"

Doc smiled sadly. "Now, see, that's the million-dollar question, Lex. It could come back any second, in a week, in a month. Who knows? If it goes beyond a week, I'd advise that she see a neurologist, though I'm not sure that one could help. I think this is more a subconscious choice than anything else." Doc looked at Trudy. "She'd been nervous about this weekend, you say?"

Trudy nodded. "Yes."

Givens grew silent for a moment. "Let's give it a week. Does she have any family, a husband we should call?"

"No," Trudy replied. "Her parents are both dead and she was an only child. If she has any other family, then I'm not aware of it."

"Okay, then," he said with a nod.

Trudy rubbed her head once more and began to pace the short length of the hall. "Oh, hell," she said, her voice filled with panic, anxiety and dread. She whirled around and faced them. "What are we going to do?" she hissed frantically at Lex, as though he were supposed to come up with the answer. "All those people will be here day after tomorrow, ready to play *To Catch a Thief.*" She groaned. "God, what a disaster. What am I going to do?" she wailed in a whisper.

Lex's heart sank. He mentally flushed his season, and the possibility of another season, down the toilet. He'd come so close to making it, had survived everything else that had been thrown at him this year, but he just didn't see any way around this, any way out of it. Dread ballooned in his belly. This was something he couldn't fix. "There's only one thing to do—you're going to have to call it off."

Her eyes widened and she harrumphed as though he'd lost his mind. "Absolutely not. That is *not* an option." She pivoted once more, clearly trying to come up with some way to salvage the weekend.

Lex blinked. Then what the hell did she plan to do? Carry on? How would that be possible, when the star player thought she was...exactly who she was supposed to be, he realized, his heart beginning to pound. It *could* actually work, Lex thought cautiously, afraid to hope, to even entertain the idea.

Trudy abruptly stopped. "Okay, we've only got a minute before she comes out, so this is what we're going to have to do." Her voice vibrated with determination. "You will have to play the part of Nash. She—"

His eyes widened. "But—"

"No buts," Trudy interrupted tightly. "She already thinks you're him. Hell, she thought you looked like him from the get-go."

So that was who he reminded her of? Lex wondered absently. Nash, the hero in her books?

"I'll play Melanie, because that has worked so far," Trudy continued. "John can handle some of the behind the scenes stuff, and fake the phone calls from Larson." She frowned thoughtfully. "The only problem that I see is her name. For the purposes of this weekend, she has to be called Zoe—her fans expect it—yet 'Zoe' believes that she's undercover." She hummed under her breath. "I don't know. I'll have to think about that. I'll figure it out." Her gaze found Lex's once more. "But you'll have to cram. Big time. Everybody here knows their part but you and, aside from Zoe, of course, you have the most important role."

Cram? Lex thought wildly. When was he supposed to cram? Hell, he barely had time to sleep.

Lex wanted this to work more than anything—he had a lot riding on it, more than the rest of them, after all—but he wasn't a fast reader and he suspected he'd be an even lousier actor. There was no way he would be able to handle this. He hated it, regretted it, but he just didn't see how he could make it work.

He couldn't be Nash Austin.

He shook his head, rubbed the back of his neck, then readied his mouth to tell Trudy this. But apparently she'd read his expression, and abruptly cut him off.

"I'll make it worth your while."

He stifled a bitter laugh. "If it was about the money, I'd say yes. But it's not. I just don't have the time, and I damn sure don't have the ability."

Besides, *playing* the part of a woman's lover was a role he simply wasn't all that comfortable with, particularly under these circumstances. What would Faith think of him when her memory returned? He mentally snorted. Hell, she'd think he was an opportunistic lecher, that's what she'd think, because if he played the part of her lover, there was no way in hell he'd be able to keep his hands off her. He'd have to have her, and his conscience simply wouldn't allow him to do it.

Trudy uttered a figure that would replace his leaky roof and then some. His conscience shut up.

Stunned, Lex stared blankly at her. "You have to be kidding."

"No, I'm not," she said levelly. The bubbly drill sergeant had vanished. "If we call this off the bad publicity would cost us a hell of a lot more. It would be disastrous." She paused. "Will you do it?"

Lex hesitated. Indecision gnawed at him. But then he imagined fixing his roof, buying a few new things for the lodge, putting a little away for a rainy day.

He imagined doling out the promised Christmas bonuses.

He imagined being able to take a deep breath out of satisfaction and relief, rather than to lessen the perpetual balloon of anxiety he carried around his gut.

It was a business arrangement, he told himself, trying to rationalize his ultimate decision. He'd have to act—actors got paid, right?

Though his conscience twinged in imaginary warning, Lex finally nodded. "Yeah, I'll do it."

Trudy sighed, obviously relieved, then smiled. "Excellent."

Faith opened the door and stepped into the hall, oblivious to the tension gathered there. "Melanie, what the hell am I wearing? I'm—" she pulled the beige sweater away from her body and looked down at herself in apparent disgust "—colorless."

"You were in disguise until we got to our location," Trudy improvised without the smallest hesitation. "Then you hit your head, and haven't had time to change."

Looking adorably confused, Faith merely nodded. "That explains that. What about my gun?"

Jesus, Lex thought and resisted the urge to do a double take. Her *gun?*

"It's back at the lodge. I've received a message from Larson," Trudy said gravely, deftly directing the conversation away from firearms. "He'll call at five for an update. Apparently, there's been a change in plans."

Faith digested this bit of information. She looked at Lex. "What about Boyle? Has he surfaced yet?"

Lex's brain froze. "Er..."

"Not that we're aware of," Trudy interjected smoothly. "You'll have to put him out of your head for the time being." She summoned a faint smile. "We have other crooks to catch."

Lex breathed a sigh of relief as this bizarre scene played out around him. That was close. Before this went any further, he had to get back and read those damn books. There was no way he'd be able to pull this off otherwise.

Faith turned and shook Doc's hand. "Thanks for patching me up."

Doc smiled. "You're welcome. You can have ibuprofen for pain, and be sure and call me if you need anything."

Faith nodded. "Certainly." Her gaze darted from Lex to Trudy. "Okay, people. Let's roll. I've got to get back and figure out what the hell is going on." She shook her gorgeous head and a disgusted breath poofed softly from between her supremely carnal lips. "I'm totally lost."

He and Trudy shared a look as she sashayed off. *Join the club,* Lex thought ominously.

"I THINK LARSON IS ON something," Zoe muttered as she disconnected. She frowned. "He doesn't sound like himself at all."

Looking somewhat startled, Melanie glanced up. "What did he have to say?"

"You were right. Plans have changed. He suspects Boyle is behind the latest theft and that the trade-off will happen here this weekend. Not Boyle himself, mind you. A couple of his lackeys. Boyle won't sully his own hands, the ball-less bastard." She blew out a disgusted breath. Heaven help that SOB when she finally put him away, Zoe thought. If it was the last thing she ever did, she'd send his worthless ass to jail, or personally sentence his unholy soul to hell.

Zoe gave Melanie a smile. "In an ironic twist, there's a *To Catch a Thief* party here this weekend. Can you believe it? It's just like Boyle to use something like this. It suits his twisted sense of humor," she said grimly.

Melanie murmured a nonsensical sound in agreement.

"At any rate, Larson has arranged for us to participate and will e-mail you the character profiles ASAP. Nash will play lodge owner, which is just as well, because he seems to know the layout quite well already." That was her man, Zoe thought, with a small smile. So efficient...at *everything*. She sighed. "As for me, Larson has arranged for me to host the festivities, and I won't require a different name, but will use my own." Zoe chewed her bottom lip, then sat down on the edge of the bed. Unwarranted fatigue weighted her shoulders. "I'm not sure that's a good idea, but Larson is in charge and I'm obliged to follow orders."

Even though she didn't particularly care for it. Zoe liked to call the shots herself. She trusted her own judgment more than anyone else's.

Nash was the only exception to that rule—she trusted him with her life, her heart, her body—*all of it.*

God, her head ached. She didn't remember falling, but the butterfly bandage on her temple was evidence that she had. Zoe had been injured on many assignments—she'd taken a bullet in Bangkok, had been stabbed in Cozumel, had sustained countless broken ribs, cuts and abrasions—yet she couldn't recall anything hurting as badly as this damn headache. She frowned. It was truly bizarre. In fact, this entire day had been bizarre.

She shook off the sensation and released a beleaguered breath. "We'll do our preliminary surveillance over the next couple of days, learn our parts. We'll also have Nash check the guest register and make sure that we put prime suspects in easy-to-monitor rooms." She took stock of her surroundings, careful to always note pertinent details, and paused as something odd struck her. "Where are Nash's bags?"

A line emerged between Melanie's brows. "I'm sorry?"

Zoe sat up once more and scowled at the room at large. "Nash's bags. I don't see them."

"Oh. He must have left them downstairs," Melanie said, and for some reason, her assistant's answer rang more like sudden inspiration than bona fide truth.

A funny feeling camped in the back of Zoe's neck, that same telling sensation she got when something didn't vibe quite as it should. Presently, though she couldn't put her finger on precisely what, something didn't feel quite...right. "I think I'll go downstairs and check it out. I need to have a look around the place, anyway."

Melanie quickly discarded her PDA and scrambled from her seat next to the window. She hurriedly smoothed her hair away from her face. "I'll, uh, come with you."

"No, that won't be necessary. You stay here and get some rest. Trust me," Zoe told her, summoning a wry smile. She picked up her gun from the bureau, then slipped it into the waistband at the back of her skirt. "You're going to need it."

Zoe easily retraced her steps down to the huge great room. Funny how crooks sometimes chose the most beautiful places to conduct their business, she thought, admiring the vaulted ceilings and exposed beams. The stacked stone and rough-cut cedar were utterly charming, inspired a cozy feeling of warmth, happiness and home. Huge braided rugs covered the worn hardwood floors and antique quilts were hung on the walls, giant patchwork pictures that added splashes of color that fit the natural decor.

Rather than drape the windows, the owner had left them bare, choosing rather to frame the outdoors, which was presently garbed in a rich tapestry of fall color. As Zoe gazed around the room, a curious feeling, one that couldn't be readily described, much less named, stole into her heart. Though this day had felt oddly peculiar, something about being in this place gave her an inexplicable sense of security.

The sound of Nash's voice drew her gaze, pushing a small *it-figured* smile to her lips. He stood behind the registration counter efficiently checking something on the computer, a cordless phone wedged between shoulder and ear. A grimace moved across his handsome face and Zoe smiled as she read a hot oath form on those incredible lips.

Just looking at him made something hot and achy stir in her loins, made her belly quiver and the breath ease out in a stutter from her lungs. A sense that was familiar yet new fluttered warmly through her chest, and she was startled to recognize the *new* as anticipation. Her heart pounded in that same frantic beat it had when she'd been desperately waiting for their first kiss, that do-or-die longing that romantics rhapsodized about in lyrics and verse.

Which was ridiculous when she and Nash had been lovers for years, had shared their bodies in acts so depraved they'd make Hugh Hefner blush. There wasn't an inch of Nash she hadn't explored, a part of him she hadn't tasted. He'd laid claim likewise to her, and yet Zoe knew tonight when they went to bed, it would feel like the first time all over again.

The mere idea sent a dart of heat straight to her womb. A tingly warmth licked her nipples and settled in her sex.

He replaced the handset, blew out a breath and passed a hand wearily over his face. Then he looked up and his startled gaze connected with hers.

Zoe smiled, resumed her trek across the room. "Hi, handsome," she murmured. His woodsy fragrance tickled her senses. She leaned forward, cupped his jaw, then slanted her lips over his. She kissed him slowly and deeply, shivered as his tongue rasped against hers. The heat that had stirred in her loins only moments before flared into an inferno that quickly melted her thighs. She decided she'd better stop now, before she got too carried away and couldn't.

She reluctantly ended the kiss. "Seems like you anticipated your part once again. You're supposed to be the lodge owner this weekend." She briefed him on the rest of the plan. "We'll finish prep work tomorrow. Once you've looked at the register and we've gone over the character profiles, we can organize our strategy."

"Sounds great," Nash murmured distractedly, seeming out of sorts. His gaze darted over her, lingering just long enough on her breasts and legs to flatter her. He tugged at the collar of his shirt. "You changed clothes, I see."

"Gad, yes," Zoe replied with a low chuckle. She'd felt like a little brown wren in that disguise-garb she'd had on earlier.

Zoe preferred classic black, and vivid colors. Reds, blues, greens and oranges, and occasionally a splash of white. She wasn't model material, but she made the most of what she had by accentuating the positive. Short skirts showcased a better-than-average set of legs, and colorful clothes compensated for her not-so-remarkable light brown hair and eyes.

Her somewhat flashy style wasn't for everyone,

but she'd certainly captured Nash's attention, and right now those ice-blue eyes radiated enough heat to make any woman feel special.

Nash swallowed. "You look incredible. As always," he added hastily. "You, uh, always look wonderful." He swallowed again, seemingly embarrassed issuing the compliment.

Amazingly, Zoe felt a blush creep up her neck. Did she blush? Had she ever blushed? Why did this feel like such an anomaly? "As do you, thanks," she murmured, cast adrift in another sea of weird. She gave her head a small shake, then winced when it hurt.

"Are you all right?" he asked, concerned. "Do you need an aspirin?"

"No, I'm fine. Look, the reason I came down was to get your bags. Tell me where they are and I'll take them upstairs for you."

"That, uh— That won't be necessary. In keeping with the ruse, Melanie has already arranged with the owner for me to have his quarters."

Zoe frowned. Now that was odd. Melanie hadn't mentioned it when she'd brought up the issue of Nash's things. "That's funny. She didn't—"

"She just called a moment ago," Nash hastened to explain, evidently reading her line of thought. He gestured toward the phone.

"Oh. Well, okay," Zoe said, still somewhat befuddled. "In that case, I'll just go get my things. Where's our room?"

Nash froze and a peculiar smile curled his lips. "O-our room?" His voice held a strangled quality.

"Yes," she said patiently. "Our room. Nothing against Melanie," she confided, "but on the rare occasions our missions coincide, I'd rather have you for a roomie." She straightened. "So where is it? I want to get unpacked, then find something to eat. It's the oddest thing, but I don't remember having so much as a cracker today."

Nash mumbled something under his breath.

"What?"

A strained smile wobbled into place. "Let's get your things, darling, and I'll show you our room."

Zoe paused, laid a comforting hand on his arm. "Are you all right, Nash? Is something bothering you?"

He shook his head. "No. I just... I just hate that bastard Larson," he said heatedly. He pounded his fist on the counter. "We have to take him down."

Her brow knitted in confusion. "Larson?"

His startled gaze swung to hers and his eyes widened slightly. "Boyle," he corrected hastily. "I hate *Boyle*."

A wisp of something teased her brain, but it drifted away before she could catch it.

Nash rounded the counter. "Come along," he said briskly, herding her toward the stairs. "We've got a lot to do. A jewel thief to catch, bad guys to take down."

"Right," Zoe muttered distractedly, suddenly bewildered. *Thieves and bad guys...*

5

"OKAY," TRUDY TOLD HIM. She peeked around him to make sure that Faith hadn't returned from the bathroom, then shoved a bundle at him. "Here are the first four books, as well as the audio versions." She peered up at him. "Do you have a Walkman?"

Lex nodded.

"Good," she continued, and breathed a small sigh of relief. "The tapes are abridged, so I've marked certain pertinent scenes in the books with mini sticky notes. Be careful with them, though, because they're door prizes. Hurry," she hissed. "Go hide them in your room, and be sure that it's a place where she won't find them." Trudy's expression turned grim. She flipped a book over and tapped the back cover. "I don't think she needs to see this. Who knows what sort of damage it might do?"

In his mind, Faith's smiling face looked up at him. She wore a bright red sweater, black leather pants and a grin that was sexy yet...strained. Those melted-caramel eyes were crinkled at the corners and glittered with warmth, humor and a hint of untold secrets.

All three got to him on a level that had no place in this ruse he'd chosen to participate in.

Though the lodge would benefit—and God knew it certainly needed it—he still had misgivings about the whole idea. To be totally honest, if he weren't attracted to her it might have been easier, might not have felt so sneaky, underhanded.

As it was, it did.

And to make matters worse, when she'd kissed him this afternoon—when those ripe, plum-soft lips had landed against his—it had been like touching a match to dry timber. He'd been set ablaze, had literally heard the fire roar in his ears, and ultimately settle in his groin. Lex had wanted before, was no stranger to attraction or desire. But what this woman inspired in just the few hours he'd been with her blew everything in his experience out of the water. She made him quake with lust, tripped some sort of internal trigger that vibrated the most primal of urges inside him. That kiss...

How in God's name was he supposed to keep his hands off her when she did provoking things like that? Lex wondered with fury and despair. How was he supposed to sleep in the same room—*same bed*—with her and not take what she would undoubtedly offer? What she would likely expect? Zoe and Nash were lovers—burned up the pages, according to Trudy. Lex ground his teeth.

The mere thought made *both* of his heads throb.

"Go," Trudy urged, yanking Lex out of his tortured reverie. "She'll be out any minute now."

Lex hurried to the bedroom—and drew up short.

Feminine clutter—clothes, shoes, makeup, various bottles of lotions and perfumes—littered the totally masculine space. Slinky undergarments were draped over his cedar chest and suspended from all but one pole of his four-poster bed. A black-and-pink garter hung from one of the antlers on the deer head mounted to the wall. His lips quirked. He seriously doubted his taxidermist would appreciate Faith's addition to his project.

The room was decorated in classic lodge style, with a color palette of black, brown, rust, green and gold. Heavy fabrics, heavy furniture and scenic pictures of mountain streams and various wildlife completed the decor.

Faith's things looked like a bouquet of spring flowers scattered among a fallow fall field. Curiously, they didn't look out of place, a fact that would ordinarily provoke further consideration, but regrettably—or thankfully; Lex wasn't sure—he didn't have the time.

He looked around the room, considered the colorful clothes strewn about and compared them to what she'd had on when she first arrived at the lodge. There'd been nothing wrong with what she'd worn—classic beige and brown—but there had been nothing remarkable about it, either. It was as if she wanted to blend in, to become a part of the scenery, not really be seen.

Whereas her flashy heroine, Zoe, clearly dressed to stand out.

For the first time since the amnesia had set in, Lex wondered about what Doc Givens had said. Was it possible that he'd been right? That the amnesia could have been brought about by her subconscious rather than the blow to the head? That Faith had been so anxious about playing the part of Zoe that a hidden part of her brain had morphed her into that person at the slightest provocation? It seemed so surreal, so out of the realm of true possibility.

Doc had also mentioned another interesting insight—that perhaps Zoe was merely an extension of Faith herself. If that were the case, then where did one end and the other begin? Why did Faith live out her adventures through Zoe? Why did she hide behind the larger-than-life character she'd created? And better yet, how did Nash fit into the pic-.

ture? Was he based on a real guy—Lex's every instinct balked at the idea—or had he merely been born of her imagination?

Lex blew out a long breath. He'd have to read the books to find out, and the sooner the better. In the meantime, he had to get back to the dining room. George would have dinner out any minute and he didn't appreciate stragglers at his table. It was disrespectful.

Evidently "Zoe" didn't deem drawers as suitable housing for her clothes, so Lex loaded all of the books and tapes into his nightstand—he'd slip in later for the first tape and his Walkman—then quickly let himself out of his room and headed back to the rejoin the group.

Since Faith would likely expect him to be with her the majority of the time, Lex didn't know when precisely Trudy expected him to listen to any of the tapes, much less read the books, but he'd simply have to find both the time and a way. He certainly couldn't go any further into this farce without preparing for it. This flying-blind-by-the-seat-of-his-pants method was completely nerve-racking. He could do without the stress.

A short bark of laughter erupted from his throat. As if anything about the next few days would be stress free. He'd likely end up sedated by the end of the weekend, that or he'd simply wander off into the woods, babbling to himself like a schizophrenic off his meds.

The mouthwatering smell of George's fried chicken teased his nostrils as he neared the dining room, triggering a hungry growl from his belly. Ahh...his favorite. Comfort food, thank God, because nothing else about the coming weekend would be comfortable.

Furthermore, this day hadn't left time for any luxuries—like lunch, Lex thought with a small laugh—and, as a result, he was starved. He could have eaten anything at the moment without the slightest complaint, but thankfully, he wouldn't have to. George, bless him, though he could be a cantankerous soul, had apparently taken pity on him and decided to compensate for a rotten day by making his favorite meal.

"Poppycock!" he heard George sputter indignantly as he neared the dining room. "Everybody likes fried chicken. It's an American staple."

A premonition of dread settled in Lex's chest as he hesitated outside the door.

"No, *everybody* doesn't," Faith replied, her tone patient yet clipped. "I do. Melanie does. But our other dining companion, Nash, I'm afraid does not. I'm sure that you've gone to a lot of trouble to prepare this fine meal," Faith added gently, competently using the old more-bees-with-honey approach. "And I assure you that we'll enjoy it, but Nash is a vegetarian."

"Then *Nash* can eat the mashed potatoes and green beans," George muttered gruffly.

Lex squeezed his eyes tightly shut and resisted the urge to moan. *Nash was a vegetarian?* It wasn't bad enough that he'd gotten sucked into this farce, would have to resist a woman who thought they were lovers—a Herculean task, to be sure, since he wanted her more than he wanted his next breath—and now—*now*—to add insult to injury, he was going to starve for the rest of the weekend? He swore silently. Repeatedly.

He heard Faith tsk under her breath. "Did you cook them with fat back?"

"Of course! How else would I cook 'em?"

"Steamed is a good choice." Humor laced her voice, drawing a reluctant smile from Lex.

George snorted, wordlessly sharing his opinion of that suggestion.

She sighed. "So the green beans are out, then."

"Then he can have mashed potatoes," George grumbled.

"He'll have to tonight," Faith said. "But when

you're preparing future meals, please keep his preference in mind."

Lex stepped into the dining room, watched his uncle snap his mouth shut. No doubt he'd been about to deliver the truth about his *true* likes and dislikes, so Lex sent him a warning glare, which he swiftly morphed into an adoring smile when he looked at Faith. And he'd been afraid he couldn't act?

"Something smells good," he said in the too hearty tones of a man trying to foil an argument.

"Your friend here just told me that you were a vegetarian," George growled. "That's the sort of thing a cook likes to know *before* he prepares the meal."

"I apologize, George," Lex said, appropriately contrite. "I should have mentioned that to you this afternoon and I forgot." Of course, it was hard to share something you didn't know, Lex thought, perturbed. He'd briefed George and the rest of the staff on Faith's accident and his new role. He'd had to, or else the coming weekend would be a disaster.

George's bushy brows folded in consternation. "Is there anything else you forgot?"

Lex barely checked the impulse to snort. Not "forgot," no, but there was plenty he was sure he didn't know. "Er, not that I can think of," he told him.

George harrumphed. "Good." Then, grumbling under his breath about ungrateful guests, he shuffled off.

Lex helped Faith and Trudy into their chairs before taking a seat himself. He looked longingly at the chicken before grimly loading his plate with mashed potatoes.

"Sorry about that, honey," Faith told him. "I should have thought to ask for a vegetarian plate for you, but," she sighed, "with the recent change to plans and adjusting accordingly, I forgot."

The apology was offhand but sincere, the kind of thing he imagined couples routinely said to one another. Though they were only a couple in this fantasy world she'd created, then slipped into, the way Lex's heart warmed at the comment made him suddenly realize that it would be all too easy to start believing it himself.

She would make it easy.

"Don't worry about it," he told her, curiously disconcerted. It was one thing to want her—lust could be rationally explained, even the instantaneous, gnashing inferno of need he'd been experiencing since he first laid eyes on her. Regardless of how powerful, it was still a healthy physical reaction. Basic chemistry. But *wanting* her, feeling that emotional tug along with the need...now that was something new, and inspired no small amount of panic.

"Melanie, did those character profiles come through?" she asked, thankfully forcing his thoughts back to the here and now.

Trudy nodded. "Yes, they did. I hooked my laptop up to the computer station in the game room and printed them off."

"Good. I'd like to get a jump on my part." She speared a few green beans. "Officiating this thing while trying to catch a thief is going to be damn difficult."

Trudy smiled reassuringly. "You'll manage. After Calcutta, this should be a walk in the park."

Faith's lips curled with knowing humor. "There is that."

After Calcutta? What had happened in Calcutta? Lex wondered, intrigued. He shot Trudy a questioning glance, but she merely mouthed *read the books.*

Trudy and Faith chatted some more, but thankfully, any time a response was required of him, Trudy would interject the appropriate comment and, other than the occasional "Boyle, that bastard!" Lex didn't contribute much to the conversation.

Instead he ate a heaping plate of mashed potatoes and about half a dozen rolls. Later tonight, he'd sneak into the kitchen and raid the fridge. He was a carnivore, dammit. He needed meat. What in the hell had possessed her to create a hero who was a damn vegetarian? Maybe Nash needed to have a change of heart about that over the weekend, Lex thought, hiding a smile.

Faith sighed and pushed her plate away. "I don't know about you guys, but I'm beat."

Trudy nodded. "Me, too. We've got a busy day tomorrow."

Lex was all for the idea of calling it a night so that he wouldn't have any more chances to unwittingly screw things up...until he realized that Faith expected him to go to bed with her. Then one anxiety replaced another and a whole new sort of tension tightened his gut. He imagined sliding into bed next to her, imagined her rolling into his arms, kissing him, enflaming him...and him having to refuse.

The Prince of Darkness himself couldn't have devised a more hellish punishment for his part in this.

Faith stood, came around behind him and kneaded his shoulders. "Geez, babe," she admonished. "You're so tense."

His shoulders weren't the only part of him that was rigid, Lex thought, and swallowed the hysterical urge to laugh. His loins were locked in a fiery pit of hell and every single cell in his body commenced a slow simmer. Those small, capable hands might have worked a little magic if he could have relaxed beneath her touch, but presently a vision of those talented hands sliding over—massaging—other parts of him had manifested behind his closed lids, and it was all he could do to keep from weeping in frustration. A vision of himself plunging between her thighs materialized behind his eyelids and he expelled a miserable stuttering breath.

She leaned down and her warm breath whispered across his ear, sending simultaneous waves of fire and ice down his spine. "I know a pleasurable way we can both relieve a little tension," she murmured suggestively. "Come on," she cajoled, her voice low and sexy. "Take me to bed…and then take me."

Sweet Jesus. With effort, Lex swallowed. "I want to check the perimeter once more, then I'll, uh, be along in a minute."

He didn't know a damn thing about checking the perimeter, but he'd heard it often enough in action-adventure movies that he hoped the excuse would fly. He held his breath and waited.

She straightened and he released a silent sigh of relief. "Sure. In the meantime, I think I'll check in with Larson and make sure there are no other developments we should know about."

She bent down and brushed a kiss over his cheek. "Don't be too long."

Lex grunted a noncommittal response, even as every nerve ending screeched with need. His rod had swelled so much it was in extreme danger of busting his zipper.

Once Faith had moved out of earshot, Trudy quirked an amused brow and said, "Check the perimeter?"

Lex shoved an impatient hand through his hair. "I couldn't think of anything else." Agitated, he shot her a glare. "I warned you that I wouldn't be good at this."

"Oh, you're doing fine," Trudy assured him. "You just need to read the books. While she's calling Larson, you should probably snag the first audio book and give it a listen while you're 'checking the perimeter.'"

He'd already thought of that, and he planned to make that job last long enough for Faith to fall asleep before he had to go back in that bedroom.

An image of her in his bed rose in his mind and it took a considerable amount of effort to beat it down.

Naked limbs. Puckered breasts and dewy curls…

No woman had ever slept in his bed. On the rare occasions he'd taken a lover, the encounters had always happened at her house, a hotel, and in the case of his first time, in the back seat of his car.

But his room was his space, his bed an intimate haven he'd someday share with a wife. His children would be conceived there. Though it was an antiquated notion, that room—that bed—would eventually be home to a wife, and he had too much respect for that future woman to sully it with recreational sex.

And now he was supposed to share it with a woman who didn't even know who he was, a woman that the Pope would have a hard time refusing, a woman he wanted with an intensity that made his knees quake. Lex swore under his breath.

George came in then and began to clear the table. He picked up a chicken leg, took a bite, then looked at Lex and groaned dramatically, with as much enthusiasm as a death row inmate enjoying his last meal. "You missed some good chicken, Mr. Nash," he teased, the crafty old bastard. "Sure you don't

want to change your mind about bein' a vegetarian?''

Lex smirked. "Not yet, at any rate.''

George shrugged. "More for me, then.''

But that had reminded him... "Is there anything
else I should know about, Trudy? Any other pertinent facts that you should possibly tell me?''

An unmistakable edge tinged his voice, but he
couldn't help it. His entire world was spiraling out
of control. He was still hungry, dammit, and his
dick had staged a relentless rebellion in his
shorts—it refused to wilt, despite the fact that the
object of his lust had left the room. Under the circumstances, feigning a good mood was simply out
of the scope of his less-than-admirable acting skills.

Despite his tone, a mischievous glint sparked to
life in Trudy's eyes. "Considering that Faith has
moved into your room, and the intimate nature of
Zoe and Nash's relationship, yes.''

He exhaled mightily. "Well, what is it?''

"You've only got one testicle.''

It took a moment for his brain to believe what his
ears had heard, and by the time he'd regained his
senses, Trudy had already begun her escape.

His dick instantly thawed. "What? *How?*''

"Book two—*Lipstick and Lies*.'' She chuckled. "It
was quite...heroic.''

"*Christ,*" Lex muttered, barely checking the urge to do a quick search and make sure both of his buddies were accounted for. So now he was a *ball-less* vegetarian? Could this get any worse? *No, no,* Lex hastened to tell himself. A tic formed near his left eye. *Don't even ask, don't even wonder.*

It would not get worse.

Things had to get better.

They had to.

Just what the hell sort of hero was she inventing? he wondered, utterly stunned, outraged on the behalf of her mutilated protagonist. What sort of twisted mind relieved the supposed hero of her stories of one of his nuts, for pity's sake? A sadistic one, Lex concluded, grimly determined to find out what made Faith tick. The answer to that lay in her books, which was all the more reason he needed to read them.

Time to cram, Lex decided, chuckling darkly. Hell, he'd need to make sure the rest of his body was accounted for, if nothing else.

6

ZOE AWOKE THE NEXT morning as the first fingers of dawn were inching above the eastern horizon. Despite the glorious display of color as the sun's first rays illuminated the mountainside, a sense of confusion and dismay had shadowed her dreams and followed her into consciousness. A frown worked its way across her forehead and she winced when it pulled her temple.

Where was she? she wondered, and for a moment, blind heart-pounding panic set in. A vision of a large yellow room with blue-and-white toile linens flashed abruptly through her mind, then fled before any particulars could fully form.

Then she remembered—the fall, the wound.

The dark room she currently found herself in made sense, and the purpose for her being here moved firmly into focus.

Zoe shifted and the character profile and instructions for this *To Catch a Thief* party she'd been reading last night crumpled beneath her. She pushed her hair out of her face. Nash's side of the bed was empty and undisturbed, indicating that he'd never returned to their room last night. Disappointment weighted her shoulders.

It wasn't the first time that had happened—occasionally he'd be forced to work while she slept—but those cases were few and far between, and he ordinarily wouldn't have missed an opportunity to take her to bed. In addition, he'd been acting quite distracted lately.

Regardless, Zoe wouldn't allow herself to take it personally, because she knew beyond a shadow of a doubt that Nash loved her. Other women might call her foolish for having so much confidence, but with Nash, that simply wasn't the case.

They were made for each other.

He adored her, doted on her, but most importantly, he respected her and regarded her intelligence with the sort of admiration it deserved. He was never patronizing or arrogant, and had even sought her advice on occasion. They were equals, and the measure of power between the two was nicely balanced.

And it didn't hurt that he was drop-dead gorgeous, Zoe thought as a slow smile slid across her lips. To be perfectly honest, he couldn't have been more perfect than if she'd designed him herself.

Nash Austin was everything a man should be.

He was handsome and fearless, intelligent and funny, loyal and honest. Those ice-blue eyes could look at her in a way so hot, it sent chills trickling down her spine. Made a deep achy throb settle in her womb, and every cell in her body hum with a desire so strong she practically vibrated from the inside out. A shiver of longing eddied through her and she slowly released a pent-up breath.

Succinctly put, he was an honorable man...with a truckload of sex appeal.

And he was all hers.

Now where the hell was he? Zoe wondered irritably. She threw the coverlet off, stood and pulled her robe from the bedpost, tied the sash, then snagged her gun from the nightstand and made her way out of the room.

Though the lodge was silent, the scent of fresh-brewed coffee emanated from somewhere deep in the house, and she suspected that George, the surly but endearing cook, was most likely responsible. Undoubtedly he adhered to the old *early to bed, early to rise* proverb, but as far as Zoe was concerned she'd just as soon stay up late and linger in bed.

She would have particularly liked to linger this morning, if Nash had deigned to join her.

She'd been inexplicably horny since they'd gotten here, her need sharper, keener, more desperate. She wanted to feel his delicious weight between her thighs, wanted to feel the hot, throbbing length of him buried deeply inside her, then clench around him as she came, the most hedonistic sensation she could ever imagine. Her feminine muscles inexplicably tightened and warmth drenched her core.

She searched the downstairs, and when that effort proved fruitless, she decided to check the porch. Nash enjoyed the outdoors.

She found him asleep in a rocker on the back porch. A set of headphones dangled from his neck and a big black dog lay sprawled at his feet. The animal looked up as she approached.

For a split second, a flash of alarm winked through her, but one look into the soulful eyes of the magnificent beast dispelled any hint of fear. Honestly, she'd never been afraid of dogs, couldn't recall being afraid of anything, for that matter. What was wrong with her?

She dismissed the sensation, and offered her hand for the requisite sniff, then smiled when he licked her palm. "Hey, big guy," Zoe murmured softly. "Been guarding my man?" Her gaze slid back to Nash and something sharp and sweet lodged in her chest, more than desire, more than lust.

The first kiss of dawn illuminated the side of his face and lent a gold tint to his boyishly mussed coal-black hair. His face was relaxed in sleep, the sharp angles and smooth planes a masterpiece of masculine artistry. Her fingers hesitated, then ultimately traced the scar at his temple—the result of one too many recon missions for Special Forces—with her finger, then smoothed a lock of hair from his forehead.

His lids fluttered softly, then opened, revealing the clearest, most gorgeous blue eyes she'd ever seen. Zoe sucked in a short breath, curiously startled, and a flash of heat brushed the tops of her thighs.

A sleepy smile curled his lips, then his eyes widened and he sat bolt upright, dislodging the dog, who yelped and, after a reproachful glance, trotted off into the woods.

Nash winced and scrubbed a hand over his face. "Oh, hell." His voice was deep, rough with sleep. Sexy.

"That's what I thought this morning when I awoke in an empty bed," Zoe told him, a wry grin twisting her lips. "The temperature dropped considerably last night. I'm surprised you didn't catch your death."

"I've been trained to be impervious to physical discomforts, remember?" he said tiredly. He wiped the sleep from his eyes.

She arched a brow. "You were also trained to never let your guard down, yet I managed to stroll right up—armed, I might add—" she indicated her gun, then tucked it beneath the sash of her robe "—and have a conversation with that dog before you opened your eyes."

His gaze bounced from the gun to her face, then he straightened as if his senses had moved to higher alert. "The dog? You weren't afraid of the dog?"

Zoe chuckled, crossed her arms over her chest. "That harmless lump of fur? Hardly. He might lick me to death, but I doubt he would do much else."

He continued to stare at her and a ghost of a smile hovered on his lips. His eyes twinkled with some curious insight he didn't appear inclined to share. "Right."

"Why didn't you come to bed last night?" Zoe asked, ignoring his odd behavior. "Were you not confident that the perimeter was secure?"

He looked away. "Er...not entirely, no."

Zoe quirked a concerned brow. "Did you see something? Hear something?"

"No," he hedged. "Just more a feeling than anything else."

She supposed that made sense. She often trusted her instincts in the same manner. Still... "Is there something I should know, Nash? Is there some sort of danger associated with this mission that Larson has shared with you and not with me?" It would be a first, but it wasn't out of the realm of possibility.

"No, of course not," Nash replied, as though the notion were ludicrous. "He has more respect for your ability than that. I just want to make sure everything goes as planned. I don't want any surprises." He shot her a sheepish look. "I guess I underestimated how tired I was."

Zoe smiled and, unable to resist, settled herself in his lap. After the slightest of hesitations, his arms closed around her, cocooning her in instant masculine warmth. Heat slithered through her limbs. She rested her head on his shoulder, breathed in the clean woodsy fragrance that was the essence of Nash, and need kindled once more.

"It's perfectly all right," she told him, letting go a contented sigh. "Even badasses such as yourself are allowed to succumb to human weaknesses every once in a while."

His soft laugh echoed hollowly against her ear. "A badass, am I?"

"Don't ever doubt it." Smiling, she nuzzled his neck, then grimaced as her chin hit something. She looked down and noticed the headphones once more. "What were you listening to?" she asked.

His hand slid slowly over her thigh, eliciting a purr of pleasure, as he gently set the rocker in motion. "Hmm?"

"What were you listening to?" she repeated. "You've got headphones around your neck."

He tensed, then released a slow breath. "Just polishing up my Chinese," he said dismissively.

Zoe hummed under her breath, looked out over the glorious vista the morning sun painted. "God, Nash, isn't it beautiful here?" She pulled in a deep breath and savored the crisp taste of autumn. "We've been all over the world, seen some of the best the globe has to offer...and yet I don't think I've ever been anywhere that a dawn has looked more beautiful. I like it here. I don't know why, but it feels...right. Does that make sense?"

He stilled beneath her and the rocker slowed for a couple of beats before he resumed its soothing motion once again. "It makes perfect sense," he murmured, his voice rough and laced with some indiscernible element. "I agree."

"You know what?" Zoe said, as an idea suddenly occurred to her. "We should get married here."

He cleared his throat. "M-married here?"

"Yeah," Zoe told him, warming to her plan. "In the fall, just like this. I know you'd wanted to get married in your church, Nash, but that opens the whole your-church-vs.-my-church with the parents. If we do it here, that eliminates that argument."

He grunted. "I suppose."

"What?" she asked, leaning forward to study him. "Do you not like it here?"

A bark of dry laughter erupted from his throat. "No, I love it here. It's perfect."

She relaxed against him once more. "Then it's settled. We're getting married here."

So, LEX WONDERED, as Faith's rump sentenced his loins to a life sentence, in what book did Nash propose to Zoe? Just exactly when, he wondered, were they supposed to get married? Not that he didn't doubt that the fictional characters were perfect for each other, he just didn't want to face the possibility of wedding a woman with amnesia who thought he was her imaginary badass hero.

He resisted the urge to howl with laughter. To

howl with frustration. Faith's curvy little body felt entirely too perfect in his arms, her head rested too trustingly against his shoulder. It was damn hard to be noble—to keep from sliding his hands over each and every delectable inch of her—when every soft breath she took simultaneously fanned a fire in his blood and resonated with blind confidence.

He'd like nothing better than to turn her around and have her straddle him, right here in this rocker, Lex thought. *Robe gaping open, slipping down her slim shoulders. Her honey curls mingling with his darker ones as the rhythm of the rocker catapulted them to simultaneous release right as the dawn broke over the mountain....*

Lex shifted, sucked in a slow breath as the fantasy played out in the private theater of his mind. God, this was madness. What the hell was he going to do? He wanted her. Desperately. Need gnashed around inside him, writhed in the pit of his belly, but there was another emotion attached to that desperate longing, one he didn't recognize and was all too afraid to label.

Because that emotion scared the living hell out of him. And it wasn't possible, Lex told himself. He'd just met her, for pity's sake. What he suspected he felt couldn't be true. It couldn't be. And yet...

He'd been drawn to her from the very beginning,

had felt a connection beyond the physical from the very first moment he'd laid eyes on her. There'd been something about her, a combination of mischief and vulnerability that had inexplicably captivated him. He'd known—he'd known on some inexplicable level—that agreeing to play this part would be difficult. Some secret sense had warned him against the idea.

And now he knew why.

Lex had listened to the first book, had been utterly hooked from the first few sentences of the story. When Trudy had told him that Faith was the best in the business when it came to romantic adventure, he'd thought she'd merely been touting her friend, possibly trying to score a few more sales.

He hadn't been prepared for Faith's sheer talent, the incredible craftsmanship of her stories.

He hadn't counted on holding his breath, waiting for the conclusion. He hadn't counted on sneaking back into his bedroom while she slept to pick up the next book on tape because he couldn't bear the cliff-hanger at the end of the first.

The storytelling was simply phenomenal, but it wasn't so much the story as the characters that moved the plot forward. Doc had been right. Zoe Wilder was simply an extension of Faith. She represented her hopes and dreams, conquered on the page fears that couldn't be eradicated in reality. She was clever and fearless, witty and charming. He grinned.

Zoe was Faith...only wilder.

Just moments ago when she'd mentioned how beautiful the mountains were—his mountain—when she'd talked about how things felt *right* here, he'd been in complete agreement with her...but for different reasons.

Having her in his arms, her sweet rump settled in his lap, the curve of her hip beneath his palm, her head upon his shoulder—*just like now*—had felt right to Lex. So right that he could barely draw a breath, and fear of screwing up what could be the most important weekend of his life filled his abdomen with gut-wrenching dread.

This woman was special.

Lex sighed. And she was in love with another man—Nash Austin.

Granted, that man wasn't real, but a fictitious character she'd spun out of thin air and into her Mr. Perfect, but she loved him all the same.

But how in God's name was a guy supposed to compete with that? Lex wondered. Admittedly, he could see where she would note physical similarities between him and her fictional hero. Their hair and coloring—even the scar near the temple—was the same. They were about the same height, with the same build, though he hesitated at saying he resembled a Greek god.

But that was where the similarities ended.

Lex wouldn't know a Glock from a Beretta, or how to deactivate a bomb, and he'd never spent a year in Asia training in self-defense. He knew nothing about computer technology, global tracking devices, artificial intelligence or how to fly a plane. He wouldn't know what to do with a bonsai plant, he damn sure wasn't interested in being a vegetarian, and the chances of him sacrificing a nut to save his lover's gerbil were slim to none. Lex inwardly snorted. Save the *world* maybe, but not a rodent.

As Trudy had predicted, the mystery behind the missing nut was solved in book two. Boyle, that slimy bastard, had beaten Zoe's housekeeper and gardener within an inch of their lives, then he'd set a bomb to blow the whole place to smithereens. Nash and Zoe had arrived in time to save them, but not in time to deactivate the bomb. So the rescue was on. Zoe grabbed the housekeeper, Nash grabbed the gardener, and they had almost made it to safety when Zoe remembered the gerbil.

Knowing how much the little animal meant to his fair heroine, Nash had doubled back—putting himself and the gardener at considerable risk worthy of a proper hero—then grabbed the gerbil and shoved the frightened animal into his pocket.

Lex winced even now, felt his nuts shrivel and hide. The gerbil had thanked Nash for saving his worthless life by sinking his teeth into one of Nash's nuts.

Lex's own man berries had shriveled up with dread while he'd read that scene. He could see where a woman might find it romantic, but a man? Nah. Practically from infancy men learned to guard their jewels. And to lose one over a gerbil?

No way.

Lex heaved an internal sigh. If that's what it took to be a hero in Faith's eyes, he was doomed to fail.

"We should probably get inside," Faith muttered, reluctantly moving to her feet. He immediately missed her warmth, the soft womanly feel of her body next to his.

"Melanie will be up soon and we'll need to coordinate our strategy and go over our profiles. I spent a little time reading through mine last night. While I was waiting for you," she added pointedly, but without any real heat.

She put her hands at the small of her back and stretched, inadvertently pushing her unrestrained breasts against the slinky fabric of her robe. The sun had made it above the mountain, backlighting her until the shadow of her lush form was silhouetted behind the thin layer of satiny material. The rounded globes of her breasts, a waist he could easily span with his hands, the perfect swell of womanly hips, toned thighs and shapely legs... Utterly perfect.

Lex's mouth grew parched, then watered. The room behind his zipper lessened to the point just short of pain, and a curious buzzing noise had commenced in his head. Probably in warning, to let him know there wasn't any blood left there, Lex thought, swallowing thickly.

Fawn-colored curls framed her piquant face in a halo of bright gold, and the rosy flush of sleep still clung to her cheeks. She closed her eyes and a faint, satisfied smile curled her unbelievably carnal lips.

He was hit with the blinding, almost irrepressible urge to kiss her. To frame her face and lower his mouth to hers, then back her against the porch railing, spread her delectable thighs and bury himself to the hilt in her sweet warmth. Anticipation pumped through his veins in a rush that made his entire body vibrate with need. He wanted to taste those lips, to feed at her sweet, wicked mouth, to feel her pebbled nipple against his tongue, taste the rich womanly nectar he'd find hidden between her legs. A fierce heat swept him from head to toe, burning up anything remotely resembling common sense.

Lex slowly stood. Being sensible was overrated. He wanted to kiss her. To have her. Had to. Right now. He reached out...

...then froze as her gun slipped from the sash and clattered to the porch.

He blinked, stunned, as though he'd been hit with an electrical current, then a litany of anatomically impossible curses streamed through his brain.

"Oh, hell," Faith muttered as she nonchalantly bent and picked up the gun, checked to make sure it was okay. She shrugged, unconcerned. "Good thing the safety was on."

Good thing Nash hadn't lost another nut, Lex thought, as the horrifying possibilities of what could have happened occurred to him. Jesus, his nerves were shot. He took a deep breath and tried to force his heart rate into a regular rhythm. He didn't have to worry about the hard-on. It had wilted and headed for higher ground with the rest of him when the gun had dropped to the porch.

"Yeah, good thing," Lex responded shakily, the understatement of the year. He had to speak to Trudy about this. Under the circumstances, he really didn't think that Faith needed to be packing heat.

He pushed a trembling hand through his hair. Hell, she inspired enough of that already.

7

"THESE INSTRUCTIONS HAVE to be followed to the letter and anyone who violates these rules will be immediately terminated from play. Understood?"

Lex leaned against the fireplace and listened to Trudy explain to the lucky winners of Faith's *To Catch a Thief* weekend how the game would unfold. Players had descended on the lodge around three that afternoon and the excitement was virtually palpable.

It was imperative that no one mentioned Faith Bonner or any of the books—he'd already rounded up every copy the players had brought along to be signed, and hidden them in the kitchen pantry— but he still wondered how Trudy planned to keep the group from blowing the ruse.

"From this moment on, you are in character." She propped her fingers together beneath her chin and issued the order in a tone that commanded Obedience or Death. "You have never read a Faith Bonner book. You have never heard of Zoe Wilder or Nash Austin. You are forbidden to bring up

Faith or any of the stories because—for this week-end—*in your new reality, they don't exist.*" She paused, letting that dramatic statement sink in. "Your character profiles were mailed to you. Did everyone receive them?"

Several participants bobbed their heads in assent, while a murmured chorus of yeses drifted through the room.

Trudy smiled encouragingly. "Excellent. I'm assuming all of you have read your profiles, but I would advise you to take the opportunity this afternoon to go over them again. Faith designed this game so that each of you could literally step into an adventure. Each of you has a key part, delivers key clues...and red herrings," she added with a small smile. "Each of you plays an integral part of this mystery. And the best thing about this game is that none of you—not even the character who unwittingly plays the thief—knows the outcome." Her eyes twinkled.

An excited hush moved through the crowd, and though he wouldn't have initially thought he would enjoy something like this, Lex found himself genuinely intrigued. Now that he knew the way Faith's crafty little mind worked, he looked forward to seeing if he could figure out who she'd made the thief, to seeing if he could solve the mystery.

"In order for everyone to have a wonderful experience, the rules have to be followed to the letter," Trudy continued. "I cannot stress that enough." She looked out over the crowd. "Are there any questions?" No one spoke. "Good," she said briskly, finishing up the instructions. "We'll meet for dinner tonight at six in the dining room, and will begin play promptly thereafter."

Lex waited for the ecstatic group to disperse, then made his way over to where Trudy was gathering her things. "You handled that well," he told her. "I'd wondered how you meant to keep from letting the cat out of the bag."

Trudy straightened and for the first time Lex noted the anxious wrinkle between her eyes. The strain of the ruse and concern for her friend seemed to be taking their toll. "I couldn't figure out any other way to make it work. If one of them slips up..." She left the rest unsaid, but Lex didn't have any problem filling in the blank. He had the same concerns.

He rubbed the back of his neck. "Doc called a little while ago to check on her."

"What does he think?"

Lex sighed. "He assured me that we're doing the

right thing, that she'll come back when she's ready."

Trudy had trouble meeting his gaze, but she finally did and a sad smile shaped her lips. "But what if she's never ready, Lex? What if she likes being Zoe Wilder better than she liked being Faith Bonner?"

Lex blinked, taken aback. Curiously, the thought hadn't occurred to him. "Surely not," he scoffed uncertainly. He frowned. "Is her real life that bad?"

Trudy hesitated, clearly torn between voicing her thoughts and sharing personal aspects of her friend's life. "Her life isn't that bad, no," she finally admitted. "But I do think it's that lonely."

Lonely? So even though Faith had based Zoe on herself, Nash had been born strictly of her imagination. Irrational relief expanded in his chest, pushing a breath he hadn't realized he'd been holding out of his lungs. "So there is no Nash in her real life?"

Trudy shook her head. "If there was, don't you think he would be here? That's my point exactly." She sighed wearily. "In this life…she has you. Why would she want to go back?"

Leaving him with that heavy thought, Trudy

walked away, citing final preparations that needed to be seen to.

For a moment, Lex stood there, rooted to the carpet.

In this life she has you. Why would she want to go back?

His heart tripped in his chest and his tongue suddenly turned to sandpaper. In the dimmest part of his mind, Lex had worried that her memory might not come back, but he'd pushed the concern aside, because, frankly, he hadn't had time to worry about it. The part of his brain that hadn't been occupied keeping this hellish attraction under control had been busy tending to the lodge, learning his role, listening to the tapes—he'd finished up the last two last night and had even managed to skim those highlighted parts of the books Trudy had given him.

But he hadn't had time to so much as think about when her memory might come back—he'd been more concerned with making sure this weekend was as successful as Trudy insisted it had to be.

With keeping his hands to himself.

Now her parting comment penetrated those other concerns and hit a bull's-eye in Worry Central. What would they do if her memory didn't come back? What the hell was plan B?

Doc Givens had said to give it a week, then consult a neurologist, but he'd been less than hopeful that one could help. What other options did that leave? Lex wondered now. Telling her the truth? Doc had advised against that course of action, yet continuing to play the part of Nash Austin was completely out of the question.

Or at least it should be.

Curiously, he didn't find the idea as onerous as he should have. Granted, being the object of Zoe's love for the past couple of days had been heartily nerve-racking, but it had also been rather...nice.

Particularly when she really was Faith.

Zoe was merely a character, an exaggerated extension of Faith, and he no longer considered the former when he thought of her in terms of a woman.

He'd been attracted to *Faith*.

To him, she *was* Faith.

The end.

And it was quite a thing to be loved by a woman like that, to be the recipient of her undivided attention. Her affection. To be catered to, respected, loved, desired. Lex sighed as a tingling sensation took root in his chest.

Powerful stuff, that.

For one insane instant, he entertained the idea of

talking "Zoe" into retiring from her action-adventure lifestyle, pretending that Nash bought the lodge so the two of them could live happily ever after on his mountain.

But then a disturbing truth surfaced and the dream vanished in a whiff of smoke—he was not Nash Austin.

No matter what she thought right now, Lex was not the man she was in love with. She was in love with a character, one she'd crafted herself, and Lex knew that he didn't have a prayer of competing with her larger-than-life hero. He didn't know how to be a hero—he was a real man, with imperfections and idiosyncrasies that would likely drive her nuts. He could be surly and impatient, overbearing and arrogant.

Simply put, he was a guy.

With guy urges.

Last night he'd waited until he knew beyond a shadow of a doubt that Faith would be asleep before heading to bed. Trudy had insisted it would be out of character for Nash to sleep on the porch again, so he'd gritted his teeth, prepared himself for a night of hell and had finally gone to his room around 2:00 a.m.

Faith had fallen asleep with the bedside lamp on. She'd been curled up on her side with a hand pillowed beneath her cheek. The other clutched the comforter tightly beneath her pert chin. She'd slung a bare leg over the top of the coverlet and a sliver of black satin and lace brushed the top of her thigh.

His breath had stalled in his lungs, his chest had contracted painfully with some unnamed terrifying emotion and, for interminable minutes, he'd just stood there, unable to move. A woman was finally in his room—*in his bed*—and if he paraded hundreds of them through here, he knew he'd never see another one who actually belonged.

She did.

And with that realization, three things hit him at once. Overwhelming peace, gut-wrenching fear and pure unadulterated need.

Then he'd stopped thinking altogether, stripped down to a T-shirt and boxers, and gingerly slid into bed next to her.

She'd murmured a nonsensical sound, something sleepy and incoherent—profoundly sexy—then instantly bellied up to his back and sighed, a breath as soft as a warm breeze. He'd tensed at first, but once he'd gotten over the shock of her lush breasts branding him, gotten past the feel of her slim leg slung over his thigh, he'd started to relax.

With a hard-on he couldn't have gotten rid of by lifting a two-ton truck. He chuckled softly.

She was the one, Lex had realized, the conclusion alarmingly swift and startlingly clear amid a mine-field of uncertainties. And somehow, after all of this was over—after she'd gotten her memory back—he had to make her his, had to try and wres-tle her love away from a figment of her imagina-tion, from a fictitious hero she'd designed herself.

An ironic chuckle fizzed up the back of his throat. *He had to have Faith.* With that thought, he'd drifted off into a deep, dreamless sleep.

FROM HER VANTAGE POINT on the second-story landing, Zoe looked at the crowd of assembled guests and resisted the depressing urge to sigh. One of these innocuous-looking, laughing, happy people was a jewel thief. One of them, under Boyle's orders, had murdered a security guard and fled with over a half-million dollars in uncut dia-monds.

That one, Zoe resolutely decided, would pay.

She shook her head. It was really such a shame that greed could lead a person to do such heinous things.

Melanie joined her in surveying the crowd. "So what do you think?" she asked.

"I think they all look innocent," Zoe replied with a grin, and it was the truth. She'd personally read over each of the *About Me* forms the participants had provided for the event, and many of them seemed entirely too normal for the character and duplicity needed to pull off such a crime.

There were a couple of retired schoolteachers, a social worker from Mississippi, a postman from Detroit, an engineer, a salesclerk, a flight attendant, a nurse and a couple of housewives. All of these people represented Middle America, the salt-of-the-earth types—but one of them was lying. Zoe frowned. It seemed utterly impossible to her that one of them was a thief. And yet her intel couldn't be wrong.

One of them was guilty.

Her job was to find that one and bring him or her to justice.

She had to keep focused. Hell, it wasn't as if the thief was going to wear a big *T* on his shirt, or brandish his loot and make it easy for her. This one had been a savvy crook, and it would take a little savvy maneuvering to unmask him, or her, as the case may be.

Zoe's lips quirked and determination stiffened her spine. Luckily, she was up to the task.

"Any one of them stand out? Seem more likely

than any of the others?" Melanie asked. She had briefed the group first, giving Zoe that much more time to study their forms and get Larson to run preliminary background checks.

"I'll know more when I meet them, but based on what I've read, I'd say the engineer and the flight attendant. Both frequently travel with their jobs, can move from country to country without suspicion. According to Larson, both have been to Colombia recently. Steve, the engineer, was on business for his company, and Gabrielle, the flight attendant, had a two-day layover during the time of the theft."

Melanie hummed thoughtfully under her breath. "Has Nash booked them into rooms that can be easily monitored and searched?"

Zoe nodded. "He has. Though he doesn't know it, I'm going to do a quick look-through tonight during dinner. I've arranged for Larson to put through a call I 'have to take,' and I'll slip away."

"Are you sure that's wise?" Melanie asked. "Shouldn't Nash go with you?"

"No," Zoe sighed. "I can work more quickly without him." Besides, anytime she and Nash came near a bed, she got ideas in her head that didn't have anything to do with catching a thief or any other bad guy, for that matter. She thought about tearing his clothes off and having her wicked way with him, a prospect she entertained even more frequently of late.

Though she hadn't gotten to relieve him of his clothes and do all the wonderfully depraved things she craved last night, at least she'd awoken in his arms this morning. She'd done it countless times before, of course. Theirs had been a long relationship, more than three years, if memory served, but for some reason waking up with him this morning had felt curiously...new.

That totally Nash scent, faintly woodsy and male, had seemed sharper, more real, and the way his masculine hair abraded her bare leg had been positively delicious. His warm, hard body had inspired images of naked limbs, sibilant sighs...hot sex. Her belly had grown all hot and muddled and her insides had commenced a low, steady simmer. Every cell in her body had been almost painfully aware of him and she'd wanted—*wanted*—more than she ever had in her life.

She'd slid her hand over his abdomen and kissed his nape....

And then George had knocked on the door, cited an emergency that required Nash's immediate attention, and she'd been left with an evil brew of lust, need and desire roiling in her belly, and a virulent case of unsatisfied longing.

For reasons that escaped her, the sensation had seemed entirely too familiar.

Which didn't make any sense, because she and Nash had always had a healthy sex life. Voracious, really. The timing thus far had simply been off, but she hoped that would soon be rectified. They'd catch this thief and carve a little time out of their busy schedules for each other, Zoe decided.

In fact, she wouldn't mind staying on here, at Oak Crest. There was something peaceful and homey, heart-warming about the place. She could *breathe* here, fill her lungs to capacity and exhale her worries away. It was a bizarre sort of connection, but a comforting one.

She liked it here.

"What do you think?" Melanie asked. "Are you ready?"

Zoe sighed, resolutely stiffened her spine. It was time to kick ass and take names. "As ready as I'll ever be. Let's do this thing."

She'd rather floss with barbed wire than fail, and she and Nash obviously weren't going to have any time together until she caught this thieving SOB.

Crooks were not permitted to interfere with her sex life, Zoe thought irritably. It put her in a bad mood.

8

"PSST. LEX," George hissed, frantically trying to covertly snag his attention.

Lex shot him an impatient glance and nodded toward Faith, who had just came downstairs and was presently working the contingent of amateur sleuths into a frenzy of frantic delight.

Though Trudy had cautioned against mentioning Faith's name, or bringing up any of the books, the fans gathered here were obviously overjoyed and generally beside themselves with happiness over meeting Faith. Wild applause had met her entrance. Since then, they'd followed her around, hung on her every word and jockeyed for her attention as though she were visiting royalty among a crowd of peasants.

His lips twisted with wry humor. Little did they know the object of their adoration was trying to discern which one of them was a thief.

She'd dressed for the part of Zoe in a slinky sequined blouse, tight red skirt and black thigh-high boots. Bright red lipstick painted that lush mouth and she'd applied her eye makeup with a dramatic hand.

Lex was just like any red-blooded American male—show him a little flesh and a pair of high heels and he'd become instantly entranced. His mind would go blank and he'd drool like a brainless pup. But to be perfectly honest, though she looked too hot for words, he preferred the softer look she'd had when she arrived.

"Lex," George whispered again, motioning wildly.

Annoyed, Lex cast another look at Faith, then reluctantly joined his uncle in the hall. "What? I need to be in there. I—"

"We've got a problem," George interrupted. His gravelly voice rang with impatience. "The Millers are here."

Lex felt his eyes widen. "What?"

"The Millers are here. They don't have a reservation, but they insist that they made one. I told them I'd have to come and check with you."

Lex passed a hand over his face and swore hotly. The Millers were regulars, a couple of aging bird watchers who usually lodged with him three to four times a year, at least once a season. They were fantastic guests and had sent him too much business over the years for him to turn them away.

Still, having them here this weekend posed a problem. He'd avoided taking any more reservations because he knew it would take his entire staff to see to the needs of Faith's party. Furthermore, his guests typically came to the mountains to enjoy a little R and R. Staying at a lodge where an invitation-only party was being held couldn't possibly be fun for other patrons. He imagined they'd find it annoying.

While he couldn't afford to turn away business, he'd decided to err on the side of caution and keep this weekend strictly about Faith and her group. In fact, he could have sworn that he'd told the Millers this already. It seemed as if they'd called.... Lex shook his head. The Millers were good people. If they said they'd had a reservation, then he'd simply made an error.

"What do you want me to tell them?" George asked.

"I..." Lex shoved a hand through his hair, looked back over his shoulder at Faith. Indecision tore at him. "They can stay, but I'll have to talk to them."

Lex swiftly located the Millers and, after they'd exchanged pleasantries, gave them the abbreviated version of present circumstances. He left out the amnesia, but stuck with the plan Trudy had used.

Margie Miller inhaled sharply. "Faith Bonner is here?" she gasped, clasping a hand to her ample chest. "Here? In this very lodge?"

Oh, hell, Lex thought. This couldn't be good. "Yes, she—"

James Miller huffed an exasperated breath and rolled his eyes at his wife. "Margie, didn't you heed a word of what the man just said? You can't call her that—you have to call her Zoe—and you can't mention those damned books. Honestly," he harrumphed.

Margie rummaged around in her purse, then pulled out *Murder and Mayhem.* "You mean like this one?"

James's eyes widened and he gasped. "For the love of God, woman, put that away!" He wrestled the book back into her bag.

"Oh, wow, I just can't believe it!" Margie's plump body vibrated with excitement. *"Her* here," she said meaningfully. "It's a dream come true. I entered the *To Catch a Thief* contest, but didn't win." Her face fell at the reminder, then brightened once more. "Nevertheless, this is just simply marvelous. It must be marvelous for you, too, Lex." She winced, patted his arm with concern. "Are things any better for you on the financial front?" she asked gently.

Lex nodded. Keeping his financial straits from occasional guests didn't pose a problem, but the Millers were frequent lodgers and had had the dubious pleasure of being here every time something had gone wrong this year. Hiding problems from them had been impossible, and he appreciated their concern.

"They're getting better, especially with the Bonner party here," Lex finally told them. "It could turn into a yearly thing, which would be wonderful."

The couple shared a look, then each gave him a warm smile. "Indeed, it would. I hope everything runs smoothly for you, you poor dear. You've had such a bad year." She tsked under her breath. "A lesser man would have sold out."

Lex shook his head. "I don't know about that, but I'm not selling." And he wouldn't. No matter what he had to do, he wouldn't sell out.

"Well, we're just thrilled to be here," Margie tittered. "Will we be in our usual room?"

He wondered how thrilled they would be when he told them the rest. He rubbed the back of his neck and summoned a smile. "Well, see, here's the thing. If you decide to stay, Faith will have to add you to her suspect list and she'll likely search your room."

Margie and James's polite expressions froze. "What?" Margie asked.

"In order to keep with the ruse of the game, to make it believable for everyone, she'll have to be suspicious of you, as well." Lex had no idea where this bullshit was coming from, but amazingly, he seemed to be getting better at spinning lies off the top of his head.

Margie and James shared an uncomfortable look. "Oh. Well..."

"I'm really sorry," Lex told them. "But I couldn't let you stay without telling you. Will it be a problem?"

They continued to stare at one another, then Margie finally managed a smile and said, "Oh, it'll be all right. It's not like she's going to find any stolen jewels in our room," she joked. James's grin was strained and he laughed heartily, as though his wife had just delivered the best one-liner he'd ever heard.

Lex continued to smile and looked from one to the other. Now that was bizarre. Granted, he'd never suspected that Faith would find any stolen jewels in their room, but now he couldn't help but wonder just exactly what she would find there. He shook the thought off, though, and returned to the issue at hand.

"Okay," he told them. "I have to get back to the party. George will get you checked in, all right?"

At their nods, Lex pivoted and made his way back into the great room. His entrance coincided with the end of Zoe's welcome speech, and he swore. Dammit, he'd needed to hear that. What if she'd shared some sort of insight he should be privy to? Granted, they'd gone over everything yesterday during their "mission briefing." Nevertheless, he felt it was in his best interests to shadow her every move. He didn't want to let her out of his sight...which was why it was very disconcerting that he'd already lost her.

Lex scowled, did a quick scan of the room, but couldn't locate her among the throng. And he should have been able to because she stuck out like an iris in a field of dandelions. Dammit. Where the hell could she have—

His eyes widened and he grunted as he was suddenly yanked backward and pinned against the wall. The startled breath he might have exhaled was forced back into his mouth as Faith fastened her lips hungrily over his. Electricity crackled over every nerve ending, starting at his toes and sweeping up his body until his scalp prickled and he shivered. Then the current turned to gooseflesh and swiftly retraced its path. That lush mouth settled deliciously over his for the long, slow haul and everything but her lips faded into insignificance. That curious sensation of becoming suddenly deaf happened once more. Sound vanished and a heightened sense of awareness took its place.

The taste of her exploded on his tongue, sweet and wicked, and, though he knew he should figure out some way to break the kiss without giving away the game, knew that when she got her memory back she'd think he was the worst sort of lecher, Lex simply didn't have the wherewithal to do it.

She'd twined her arms about his neck, slid her hands into his hair, and her small, curvy body was melted into his as though the heat of the kiss had softened every bone and muscle inside her.

While every other part of him had gone boneless as well, there was one part that had grown instantly hard. His dick strained behind his zipper as though she were a witch and it one of her devoted familiars. His hands had been fisted at his sides, and he lifted them now, then hesitated as lust and nobility duked it out in the ring of his weakening conscience.

Her pearled nipples raked his chest, delivering nobility a knockout punch.

Lex growled low in his throat, lifted his hands to

cup her face, then slid them into her hair and angled her head to deepen the kiss. She responded instantly and her purr of pleasure resonated in his mouth.

He found himself at once enflamed and content. He could have kissed her forever, could have fed at her mouth and never required another morsel of food. Hunger of a different sort coiled in every muscle, locked him in a state of mindless arousal. Her tongue curled over his, once, twice, then suckled at his bottom lip. His knees weakened. Though he wanted to devour her, he let his hands drift slowly over her slim back, shaped her tiny waist, then cupped her rump and lifted her more closely to him.

She squirmed in his arms, desperately trying to get closer, when they couldn't have gotten a pebble between them with a jackhammer.

From somewhere in the sluggish recesses of his mind, Lex heard a throat clear dramatically, then a series of gasps and knowing chuckles.

Evidently, Faith heard it, too, because she slid slowly down and reluctantly withdrew her mouth from his. She looked up and her gaze tangled with his. A curious mix of wonder and confusion cluttered those melted-caramel orbs and she touched her fingertips to her lips as though uncertain whether to believe what had just happened between them.

In the next instant, though, she blinked the sentiment away—so quickly, in fact, he was strongly inclined to believe he'd imagined it—then laid her head upon his chest and smiled at the crowd gathered around them. "Everyone...meet Nash Austin."

More whooping and hollering ensued at this theatrical announcement, but Lex couldn't appreciate it at all because his stomach had just turned to lead.

Nash Austin.

Not him. A bitter laugh stung the back of his throat, and with effort, he swallowed it. God, he was an idiot.

George announced dinner and in a matter of seconds the throng had dispersed and adjourned to the dining room. Lex lagged behind, trying to tell himself that it was unreasonable for him to be irritated, or angry—but not hurt, dammit—just annoyed that, while the kiss had been all too real for him, for Faith it had merely been one of many she'd shared with her fictitious lover from her fantasy.

He'd discovered that Trudy's description of Nash and Zoe's sexcapades had been dead-on. To his absolute astonishment, he'd fought a hard-on every time the two of them made love in the books.

He could see Faith in the role and cast himself as her lover, and suddenly, it was *his* mouth suckling at her breast, *his* body pumping furiously in and out of her. She was murmuring those suggestive phrases to *him*, taking *him* in her mouth, delivering *him* to gut-wrenching, back-arching, silent-screaming, earth-shattering climaxes.

Him—not Nash.

"Earth to Lex?" Trudy waved her hand inches from his face. "Are you all right?"

He nodded jerkily. "Yeah. Sure," he lied. Hell, in for a penny, in for a pound. This entire weekend had been one big lie. What was another?

Trudy studied him for a moment, and something in that too perceptive gaze made him want to fidget. A faint smile finally curled her lips. "You're a good guy, you know that, Lex?" she said softly. "You're a real hero. Don't ever doubt it."

"Thanks," he muttered, startled at the compliment.

She darted a quick glance over her shoulder, then lowered her voice. "Look, I thought I'd better give you a heads-up. Faith is going to slip away during dinner and search a couple of rooms. You might want to keep a close eye on her."

His head jerked up. Shit. *And that concludes the pity party*, Lex thought with a grim smile as he hurried into the dining room. He hoped to God he wasn't too late.

ZOE SLIPPED THE MASTER key Nash had given her back into her skirt pocket, then swiftly retraced her steps down the hall. Well, that had been a monumental waste of time. Neither of her prime suspects had been in possession of anything suspicious. Zoe had checked their cell phones for recent incoming calls and numbers dialed, she'd thumbed through their wallets and checked for alternate IDs, had sifted through drawers and toiletries, and had even checked to make sure that nothing had been hidden in the soles of their shoes.

She'd learned the flight attendant had abysmal taste and a yeast infection, and that the engineer suffered from Tourette's syndrome. He'd had a how-to-cope book hidden away in the back pocket of his luggage. Nothing useful, dammit.

A noise at the end of the hall snagged her attention and she instinctively ducked into an alcove.

"You're sure it's hidden well?" a man asked. "You're sure they won't find it? Any of it?"

Zoe's senses went on red alert. She dared to peek around the corner and saw an older couple, mid-sixties maybe, waddling down the hall. Both wore their graying hair in a short, no-fuss style; both had on walking shorts and orthopedic shoes. They could have been her grandparents...if she'd had any. Did she have any? Zoe suddenly wondered, jarred by the strange thought. How weird. She had absolutely no recollection of any family. None. She winced as a sharp pain suddenly throbbed in her temple. How—

"I'm sure, James," the woman scolded. "Stop worrying. We've gotten really good at hiding our stash. No one is going to find it." A surprisingly girlish giggle sounded. "I'm the only one who wants in your pants, you old coot. As for the other, they won't know what they've found, even if they manage to locate it."

Bingo, Zoe thought, everything else forgotten. She smiled, waited patiently until she was sure they'd made it downstairs, then quickly let herself into the room they'd exited.

A quick survey showed that the couple were neat and orderly. Matching I Love Bird Watching caps were hung on either side of the dresser mirror. Socks were folded and tucked away in drawers, toiletries marched across the bathroom vanity in a regimental line, and each hanger in the closest had been spaced precisely two fingers from its neighbor. Luggage had been emptied and stowed, and pill keepers and glasses sat on each of the nightstands flanking the bed. The TV remote control had been carefully placed on the woman's side, next to her pink bifocals. Two guesses as to who wore the pants in this family, Zoe thought with a wry smile.

Speaking of pants...

She quickly patted down each pair of the man's trousers and hit pay dirt with the last pair—multi-pocketed carpenter pants—in the very back of the closet. Her spirits sank when her search didn't turn up the missing diamonds, but what she did find shocked the living crap out of her.

Fleece-lined handcuffs, a cat-o'-nine-tails whip, a spiked dog collar with chain, a bondage rope and a flogger. She'd found every kind of condom imaginable tucked away in their binoculars case—ribbed, studded rough riders, glow in the dark.

After only the smallest hesitation, Zoe pocketed a few of the plainer ones. She didn't remember if she'd packed any, and she was in too sad a shape to hear that Nash hadn't. If they didn't make love tonight, she'd lose her mind.

Especially after that mind-blowing kiss this evening. Zoe's lips tingled as she remembered, and a slow, steady throb kindled below her navel. This morning when they'd been interrupted, she'd wanted to weep. She was absolutely desperate for him, *had* to have him immediately.

The insistence that it had to be *now* couldn't be reasoned with, bargained with.

Zoe had wanted Nash before, had felt as if she would burn up from the inside out if they didn't make love, but nothing in her past experience could compare to the furious need she presently endured. There was an urgency she couldn't account for, a clamorous, all-consuming compulsion that dogged her every step, shadowed her every thought. Made her crazy.

That's why she'd dragged him out of the great room, shoved him against the wall and launched herself at his mouth. She'd been desperate, yes, but a part of her had wanted to punish him for not being as desperate as she was. He wanted her, she could tell. Those ice-blue eyes heated with smoky arousal every time he looked at her. His gaze frequently dropped to her mouth, lingered, then trailed over her breasts and belly like a silent caress, and she never walked away without feeling that hot stare on her ass.

He had to learn that he couldn't look at her like that, then not follow through with what those slaying glances implied.

But a funny thing had happened when she'd kissed him.

All of that anger and angst had sizzled away like

water on a hot griddle the moment her lips had touched his.

Though she'd kissed him countless times, though she knew how he tasted, every nuance of his body language, every hair, freckle and mole on his glorious body, for reasons she couldn't comprehend, kissing Nash this time had felt completely different. More real, sharper, keener...better. In fact, it had felt like the first time, when it hadn't been. Not even the first time this weekend and yet... Zoe stilled, marveling over the notion, then abruptly shook herself and got back to the work at hand. She still had one more thing to search—the couple's briefcase. She'd found it stowed behind the AC return. She quickly picked the lock, then sifted through the papers stored inside. There were pictures of Oak Crest in every season, as well as detailed information about the lodge—square footage and all that. She also found two boxes of coarsely ground salt. Her brow furrowed. How peculiar. Why would they need to hide their salt? What would make them—

Nash poked his head into the room, startling her from her pondering. His face wilted with relief. "Zoe, you've got to get downstairs. People are asking for you." His gaze landed on the bird-watcher hats and his eyes widened, then he spied the open briefcase across her lap. "Christ, this is the Millers' room. Put that away," he hissed. "We've got to go."

"Who are the Millers?" Zoe asked. Her radar was humming.

"A couple of regulars, according to George. They aren't part of the festivities. In fact, they just got here."

"I know," she told him. She stood and quickly stowed everything she'd discovered, making sure that the room was how she'd found it. "That's suspicious in and of itself. I'm not convinced that they have anything to do with the theft, but everyone is a suspect until we rule them out. And something doesn't feel right about the two. I found salt in their briefcase. I'm going to have Larson do a background check."

Nash scanned the hallway to make sure it was clear before they exited the room. She thought she saw his lips quiver. "Salt in their briefcase? Why is that suspicious?"

"Because that's no place to carry salt. It doesn't make any sense. We have to look at the bigger picture, Nash. You know that."

"Right," he replied. Humor danced in his blue eyes. "Did you find anything else?"

"I didn't find the missing jewels, if that's what

you mean...but I did find something of interest."
Zoe grinned.

"Oh?"

They hesitated at the landing and she pulled the condoms from her pocket and spread them like a prized hand of poker for him to see. "Yeah. I found these."

Nash's eyes bugged. He peeked over the railing, then hurriedly snatched them from her fingers. "You stole—" He lowered his voice. Squeezed his eyes tightly shut. "You stole their condoms?" he asked in an incredulous whisper.

Zoe laughed at his outraged expression. "Trust me, they'll never notice. They have plenty."

"Jesus," Nash croaked, shoving the hot prophylactics into his front pocket. "You didn't take anything else, did you?"

"No." She slid him a sidelong glance. "Though I have to confess, I had a hard time putting the handcuffs and flogger away."

His eyes widened and his jaw dropped in astonishment. "Flogger? Hand—"

Chuckling under her breath, Zoe fisted her hands in his shirt and dragged him to her once more. She rubbed herself against him, licked a hot path up the side of his neck, nipped at his ear, then slid her tongue around the tender shell. A shiver quaked through him. "If you don't take me to bed tonight," she growled teasingly, "I'm going to borrow them, cuff you to the bed and spank you."

Zoe released him, then skipped down the steps, leaving him stunned on the landing. "Don't lose those," she called over her shoulder. "We're going to need them. Tonight."

9

HOURS LATER, Lex stood in the shower and let the hot water pound some of the tension from his shoulders. What a damn nightmare, he thought tiredly. He rolled his shoulders, popped his neck. Keeping Faith out of trouble, tending to the day-to-day operations of the lodge and keeping his ever-weakening libido in check were taking their toll.

The *To Catch a Thief* kickoff had gone extremely well. But then, how else could it have gone with Trudy in charge? Honestly, the woman thought of everything, and a lesser person might have snapped under the strain of recent events, but Faith's assistant had handled things beautifully.

The players were happy with their accommodations, with the food and most especially with the game. The festivities had lasted for hours, and the only complaint that he'd heard had been that the night had come to an end too soon. It had ended with a dramatic flourish, with Zoe having two key suspects in mind.

Play would resume immediately following

breakfast tomorrow morning and continue all day. Tomorrow night would end with a red herring and the true thief would be revealed Sunday morning—he hoped to God "Zoe" kept her gun holstered. Brunch and a book signing would follow.

When asked, Trudy had confessed she had no idea how they would handle the book signing if Faith's memory hadn't returned. Lex imagined she'd fabricate some sort of emergency and leave. The fans would be vastly disappointed, but Doc Givens had stressed that her memory needed to return of its own accord—that she needed to make the conscious decision to return on her own. Who knew what sort of response seeing those books would trigger? Trudy said she simply couldn't take the risk.

"Zoe" and "Melanie" were presently comparing notes, strategizing—hell, they were probably tossing everyone's car, Lex thought with a weary chuckle—and George, bless his old soul, had organized the cleanup and had insisted that Lex take a few moments to "get his shit together." He'd delivered that order with a disapproving scowl that let Lex know he'd gotten wind of the kiss.

But just what the hell did George expect him to do? Lex wondered, mildly annoyed at the implied censure. She'd kissed him. What was he supposed to do? Tell her not to?

Number one, he'd have to be *dead* not to respond.

Number two, he'd agreed to play this part and that meant kissing her when the need arose.

He wasn't inviting her advances, and she was simply acting in the way that the character she believed she was would behave. She was Zoe, he was Nash. They were lovers. Just exactly what was he supposed to do differently?

Lex sighed, braced his hands against the shower wall and hung his head. There was nothing he could do but play along.

And his initial misgivings were nothing compared to the ones he had now.

Lex hadn't wanted to participate in this farce because he'd been attracted to her. Because, regardless of what Doc said, it felt dishonest. He couldn't help but feel he was taking advantage.

But presently his misgivings were taking a more personal turn. He grimly suspected he'd fallen for Faith. There'd been something about her from the very beginning that had called to him, something that told him this woman in particular was special. He'd been instantly enchanted—and turned on— by that dry, self-deprecating smile of hers. That clever, humorous twinkle in those pale brown eyes.

Faith was every man's secret fantasy—she was a good girl with a wicked streak, a tantalizing, impossible-to-resist combination. She was the sort of woman a man could feel comfortable with, unburden his soul to, laugh with, weep with and love. In addition, she possessed a truckload of sex appeal, and a devilish, uninhibited glint in her eye that told a man she could, without the smallest hesitation, rock his world.

The mere idea sent a bolt of heat straight to his groin.

Which brought up another issue—tonight.

A short unexpected laugh burst from his throat. She'd stolen condoms from the Millers.

From the Millers...who'd been worried about their S&M stash being found.

His bran-eating bird watchers were into the S&M scene, Lex thought, utterly astounded. A broken chuckle erupted from his throat. He shook his head, unable to make that compute, incapable of reconciling one image with the other, which, when you thought about it, he decided, was probably for the best. Who wanted to carry that picture around in their head, anyway?

At any rate, the fact that she'd taken a handful of their condoms, combined with her parting we'll-need-them-tonight comment, told him that he'd run out of excuses to avoid going to bed with her. He'd slept on the porch, he'd waited her out, he'd had George contrive emergencies. Lex had done everything, short of leaving, to avoid what would undoubtedly happen tonight.

And yet he couldn't recall ever dreading going to bed with a woman before.

Did he want her? More than he'd ever wanted anything in his life. His loins had been locked in a perpetual state of arousal since the first moment he'd laid eyes on her. Lust had been his constant companion. In his dreams, he'd made love to her in every imaginable position, some of which he suspected were anatomically impossible. He'd been on top of her, behind her, beneath her, beside her. But always with her—Faith.

But every other time he'd made love to a woman, that woman had known who *he* was. They'd alternately whispered and shouted *his* name. Tonight he would take Faith to bed, and God knows he would revel in every single minute of it, but he'd be making love to her...while she would be making love to Nash.

Every part of him rebelled at the idea.

He wanted her to want *him*.

To want to make love to *him*.

To say *his* name.

Lex blew out a breath and turned off the shower. And he might as well want the moon, because that would never happen.

When Faith finally got her memory back, she would not look upon him as the hero who'd saved her *To Catch a Thief* weekend. She would not believe that he'd had her best interests at heart, that he'd followed Doc's advice, Trudy's advice. Faith would feel betrayed, and she would ultimately despise him.

Which would make it doubly hard for him to make her love him.

From this moment on, Lex decided, every word he uttered to her that didn't pertain to playing this game would be the truth.

No more lies.

When her memory returned, she would have to look back and remember his sincerity in that regard, if nothing else.

He pushed the somber thoughts aside, wrapped a towel around his hips, then strolled to the dresser in the bedroom to retrieve a pair of underwear.

The back of his neck prickled.

"You won't be needing those," a sexy feminine voice said from the bed.

Lex squeezed his eyes shut, pulled a stuttering breath into his lungs, then slowly released it. Then he prayed for restraint, for any sort of divine inter-vention, because it would take an act of God to keep him from making love to her.

He turned around...and every bit of the saliva evaporated from his mouth. Faith wore a sheer black lace body suit that covered her from neck to toe, but clung to her form like a second skin. For all intents and purposes, she was nude...yet she wasn't. If he'd ever seen anything sexier in his life, he couldn't recall. It was scandalous, and only a woman with a perfect body could wear it, because any imperfection would have been impossible to hide.

But Faith was perfect.

Her breasts were high and round, her belly flat and trim, with virtually no waist to speak of. It was tiny, which accentuated the womanly swell of her hips, her firm thighs and toned legs. She'd painted her nails bright red, and the color contrasted sexily with the sheer black suit. The material shadowed her rosy nipples, shaded the thatch of light golden curls at the apex of her thighs.

He swallowed convulsively in a vain attempt to moisturize his mouth.

His gaze slowly drifted over her, before he fi-nally let it settle on her face. Just the smallest hint of vulnerability clung to her come-hither smile, haunted those gorgeous melted-caramel eyes, and it was that little bit of weakness, of uncertainty, that he ultimately found irresistible.

No more lies, Lex reminded himself.

"You, uh... You look absolutely stunning," he finally managed to say. The compliment came out in a strangled croak, but the message seemed to please her because her soft mouth curved into a thankful smile.

Her gaze skimmed over his chest, down his abdomen, lingered on the front of his towel, then eventually back up again. Those gorgeous eyes had darkened with desire and twinkled with humor. "So do you." She rubbed a hand over the coverlet in front of her. "But you should probably join me over here. I'd like to do a closer inspection."

A short bark of laughter burst from his throat. A closer inspection? Her closer inspection would undoubtedly kill him. "Is that so?"

She nodded. "And you have my permission to conduct a similar examination on me."

The final nail in his coffin, Lex thought, as he slowly made his way over to the bed. She rolled onto her back, forcing her breasts against the see-through material, then cocked her head and gazed at him through lowered lashes. Lex slid a hand over her calf, up her thigh as he lay down beside her.

She purred at his touch, shivered, and he felt those wordless indications of pleasure hiss through his blood, settle in his loins.

He trailed a finger slowly over her belly, then, breathing unsteadily, brushed the underside of her breast. Before his eyes, her nipple budded tightly, and it seemed the most natural thing in the world for him to bend his head and suckle her.

A startled gasp escaped her. Then she sighed and arched, pushing the globe farther into his mouth. Lex felt her fingers slide into his hair, knead his scalp. He laved her nipple, then blew, then suckled again, this time deeply, flattening the rosy peak against the roof of his mouth.

Her belly deflated as another sharp inhalation sounded, then her hands were all over him, enflaming him. Soft and warm, they slid over his hip, up his side to his shoulder, back into his hair. Then she arched up, and her hot mouth tugged at his earlobe, then blazed a trail over his neck. She tugged him away from her breast and kissed him, wildly. Deeply. As though a fever had taken hold and the rest of the world had faded into insignificance. The hot seek and retreat, the desperate plunge of her tongue in and out of his mouth stoked a fire in his belly that swiftly raged into an inferno in his groin.

His dick jerked beneath the towel, grazing her hip. She whimpered, then shifted her own hips toward his, a silent plea for release.

Sweet Mother of Jesus.

Lex let his hand wander slowly toward her sex. He drew lazy figure eights, doodled around her belly button, then slowly brushed the fabric over her curls.

She shivered once more, moaned and sank her teeth into her bottom lip.

He stroked her again, felt the moist fabric beneath his fingers, her feminine tears of desire. He wanted to taste those tears, wanted her to weep more for him. He kissed his way down her body. Licked a determined path from her neck to her breast, where he lost himself once more.

He suckled and stroked, because he wanted her mindless with need, blind to everything but him and the sweet music he played upon her body. Though he'd by no means grown bored, he worked his way farther down, swirled a path around her belly button, then farther still until he reached the feast awaiting him between her spread thighs.

Her rich womanly scent stole into his nostrils, sweet and musky. Mouthwatering.

He fastened his mouth upon her.

Faith gasped, bucked gently beneath him. Her thighs went rigid...then slowly fell farther apart, opening for him.

Lex smiled against her. "Mmm. You taste so good." He lapped at her, drew his tongue against the fabric, rubbing her in deliberate methodical strokes.

Her hands fisted in the sheets, her neck arched, and soft mewling sounds bubbled from her throat. *"Oh, God... Oh, please..."* Her head thrashed back and forth, and she tipped her hips toward his mouth, desperate for more as her body rushed headlong toward release. He could feel the tension building, could taste it on his lips. He spread her folds and latched on to her clit, sucked the tiny nub through the lace and rapidly worked his tongue against her.

Her body suddenly bowed off the bed and she screamed as the orgasm broke over her. Lex licked her, once, twice, three times, milking her quivering flesh of every last ounce of the climax.

Faith's chest heaved with exertion. "That was— I don't—" Her gaze tangled with his and she smiled. "That was amazing," she breathed reverently.

Lex discarded his towel, then reached into the

bedside drawer and fished out one of the rubbers Faith had lifted from the Millers. Tension had gathered in every muscle of his body, and it was all he could do to keep himself in check. The next time she came, he wanted to come with her. He couldn't wait to feel the greedy clench of her body wrapped around his rod. Couldn't wait to sink into her heat.

He tore into the package with his teeth, then withdrew the condom and swiftly rolled it into place. "Yeah...but it gets even better."

Then he reached down and undid the two snaps at the crotch that held her garment together, swept the fabric aside and positioned himself between her thighs. He drew back and—

A loud knock sounded at the door, followed by George's desperate voice. "Nash! Nash! Come quick!"

Lex swore hotly. Repeatedly. He gritted his teeth, and though it took every ounce of strength he possessed, he moved away from her. He shot Faith an apologetic look, then grabbed his mangled towel and fastened it around his hips. A flurry of movement behind him told him that Faith was trying to cover herself.

He opened the door a fraction. "What?" he snarled.

George's breathing was labored, his face white. "You've got to come quick. Pooh's back."

A stream of profanity flew from Lex's lips. Dammit. "I'll be there in a minute." He discarded the condom, then shoved his legs into his jeans and picked a T-shirt up from the floor.

"Pooh?" Faith asked. Her brow wrinkled in confusion. "Who's Pooh?"

Oh, Christ.

Faith.

Lex crammed his bare feet into his shoes. "Zoe, you have to stay in the house. Do you hear me? Do not, under any circumstances, come outside. This is a lodge problem, not a jewel-thief problem, I swear." His gaze bored into her. "Promise me."

Looking utterly bewildered, completely un-Zoe-like, she nodded. Her hair was mussed, her lips swollen from his kisses. Something light moved into his chest, but he didn't have time to heed or dissect it.

Instead, he quickly kissed her forehead. "I love you," he murmured. "I'll be back soon."

And it wasn't until he reached the back porch that he'd realized what he'd said, or how matter-of-fact and natural uttering those words to her felt.

And with that realization came another more startling revelation—they were true.

HE LOVED HER.

Zoe sank against the bed and let that singularly profound thought flutter around her brain like a butterfly looking for a place to alight. A warm, buoyant, tingly feeling mushroomed in her chest, and amazingly, her eyes watered. A feather of memory floated through her subconscious, but irritatingly hovered just out of reach, so she abandoned it for a more pressing thought.

He loved her.

There was something utterly magical about this moment, something that she should comprehend, but for whatever reason didn't. She'd always known that Nash loved her. It had been a given. But had he ever said the words? Had he ever lent voice to that sentiment? Annoyed, she knitted her brow. She should know this, Zoe thought, agitated. A woman didn't forget when a man professed his love. It was one of those unforgettable moments, like your first kiss, your first crush. There were some things one simply didn't forget and this should be one of them.

Furthermore, a woman should remember when a man gave her an orgasm, and though she knew that Nash had treated her to plenty of those over the years, tonight marked the first night she had a point of reference for the bone-melting event. Her body flushed with heat, recalling it. *Those big talented hands on her body, his tongue anchored to her breast, then later...to her sex.* Her thighs burned and a shiver of remembered heat tingled in her womb.

She'd been utterly desperate for him to fill her, for him to settle himself firmly between her thighs and push that hollow, achy feeling out of her gut. She'd watched him smoothly roll that condom into place and she'd literally licked her lips, she'd been so hungry for him. Her belly had trembled at the sight of him.

Six and a half feet of rock-hard, perfectly sculpted muscle and bone. Her gaze had wandered over the impressive landscape of his chest, down those six-pack abs, and settled on the jaw-dropping staff standing so proudly—so enormously—that it completely obscured his belly button.

Then, just when she was about to get her wish, George had interrupted—again.

Zoe flung herself back onto the bed and moaned miserably. Though she knew it was unreasonable, she'd begun to wonder if the little old man was taking some sort of perverse joy in wrecking her love life. But to give him credit, he'd sounded genuinely worried about...Pooh. Again, that wispy thought swirled around her brain, forcing her to shake her head in frustration when she couldn't coax the memory forward.

Something was wrong with her. Off. Out of sync. She didn't know what, but instinctively knew all wasn't as it should be. Zoe sighed.

Regrettably, she was no closer to discovering the problem than she was to discovering this jewel thief.

Tonight had gone a long way toward eliminating suspects, but unfortunately she wasn't really any closer to being able to point one out as the culprit. She had strong suspicions, grounded in data she could trust, but regardless of that intel, something about it didn't quite jive. She made a mental note to keep a closer eye on the bird watchers—there was more to them than met the eye, she was sure of it. Besides, if innocuous old couples like them were capable of being into S&M, then anyone could be the thief.

Who knew? She'd figure it out. She always did. In Zoe's opinion, there was no such thing as a smart crook. They invariably slipped up and made a mistake. The trick was being clever enough to catch it, then devising a plan that would bring them to justice.

Zoe yawned as fatigue dragged at her lids. She stood, got out of her vamp suit and into a nightie, then slid into bed. After a moment, she scowled sleepily, then sat up and swapped pillows with Nash.

His scent lingered and she found it oddly comforting.

10

LEX EXHALED A WEARY breath. Faith's party had just finished with dinner and had moved into the great room to resume play. They'd been at it all day, yet the group seemed far from weary of the game. She'd designed the event much as she would a plot, he supposed, with each intermission and mealtime coinciding with some sort of cliff-hanger or dramatic revelation. All the participants had thrown themselves into their roles, dressing as their respective characters, and an excited sort of tension hovered in the air.

To his unease, the Millers had drifted into the room to watch, but rather than politely asking them to leave, Faith/Zoe had made a grand show of inviting them to play. They'd been thrilled, of course, Margie in particular. Her doughy face had creased into a rapturous smile, and Lex could feel her happiness all the way across the room.

Little did they know Faith had an ulterior motive for the invitation. Lex suspected the Millers had the unfortunate distinction of being her prime suspects.

He'd shadowed her all day, had stood watch while she'd searched the remaining players' rooms—a nerve-racking experience to be sure. He'd had to resist the urge to pat her down every time she came out of a room, lest she decide to lift anything else from his unsuspecting guests. Thankfully, it looked as if the condoms were a one-time incident.

A pity they'd had to waste one last night, Lex thought, still locked in the miserable jaws of unre-lieved sexual frustration. By the time he'd taken care of Pooh—gotten him out of the garbage and back off into the woods—the first fingers of dawn had been clawing their way over the horizon.

Since George had been up all night, as well, and would have to help oversee breakfast, it hardly seemed fair for Lex to go back to bed. There'd been little point, anyway. He wouldn't have been able to sleep, not with Faith lying there beside him and the image of himself poised between her sweet thighs burning a hole in his retinas. As far as Lex was con-cerned, walking away from Faith in that moment should qualify him for sainthood.

Nevertheless, that was the best almost-sex he'd ever had in his life, Lex thought with a wry grin. A snake of heat stirred in his belly and his gaze turned inward as a vision of Faith in that sheer black suit, sprawled out on his bed, rose in his mind's eye. Butterscotch curls, heavy-lidded gaze, red lips, rosy nipples...

He pulled in a shallow breath and exhaled slowly. She'd been so responsive, had tasted so good. Every bit of her. He'd been so blinded with lust, he'd basically hit the high spots and had neglected other areas, a tragedy he would rectify at the first opportunity.

Though Lex knew he shouldn't make love to her, though he knew that when her memory returned she'd more than likely hate his guts, he could no longer deny that being with her was inevitable...especially after last night.

It was more than lust, more than desire, more than the primal urge to plant himself between her thighs. He'd fallen in love with her. At some point over the weekend, or possibly from the first moment he'd seen her—hell, who knew?—she'd unwittingly captured his heart.

Which hardly seemed fair, because when her memory returned, Lex knew that she'd break it.

He was not Nash Austin.

He couldn't be Nash Austin.

He would never be Nash Austin.

He was just a regular Joe who loved her and, given her penchant for heroic gestures, he knew that would never be enough.

But it wouldn't keep him from trying. After all, Faith was a once-in-a-lifetime woman, and he wasn't about to give her up to an imaginary lover, badass or no.

Tonight when he made love to her, he'd see to it that *that's* what she'd remember. A living, breathing, real man.

Her man, for the taking.

"MELANIE, I HAVE A BAD feeling about this," Zoe said grimly as she watched the last of the suspects leave the room. She helped herself to a cup of coffee from the refreshment table. "Want some?" she asked.

Melanie nodded. "Yeah, I do. It'll probably keep me up all night, but it's the best coffee I've ever had." Zoe handed her the cup and she took a sip, then moaned appreciatively. She stared at the dark brew. "Wonder where George gets it?"

Who knew? Zoe thought, or better yet, who cared? She had a thief to catch and time was swiftly running out. Tomorrow morning they would un- mask the fictional thief, and quite possibly during the festivities the real thief would get away. She rubbed her forehead, trying to push back the headache forming there.

Melanie cradled her coffee cup between her palms and curled up on one end of the sofa. "What do you have a bad feeling about?"

Releasing a pent-up sigh, Zoe lowered herself into one of the leather wing chairs next to the fire. "I don't think that the housewife is the thief. Something about it doesn't feel right."

"But she has Colombian contacts," Melanie replied. "Her brother is on mission there."

"Be that as it may, I don't think she's the one. Whoever is behind this has done an excellent job of concealing their identity."

Melanie's brow folded in dismay. "You didn't find anything when you searched the rest of the rooms?"

Zoe shook her head. "Not the first thing, nor in their vehicles, either."

Melanie's eyes twinkled and Zoe could have sworn she saw her lips quiver behind her coffee cup. "You, uh...you searched their cars?" she asked lightly.

"Yes, of course." She huffed an exasperated breath. "I found plenty of French fries, gum wrappers and soda cans, but not the first diamond."

"They're awfully small," Melanie commented sagely. "Easily concealed."

"I know, and I've taken that into account. I did a thorough search, which wasn't easy, by the way," she added with a wry quirk of her lips, "since Nash insisted on 'standing guard' for me and kept hissing at me to hurry up." Damn his gorgeous hide, Zoe thought fondly. Weird that she should find that so adorable, but she did.

If nothing else good came out of this weekend— if by some chance they didn't find the real thief—at least she and Nash had connected on a deeper, more intimate level. Somewhere over the course of their relationship she'd obviously lost sight of just what he meant to her.

In the beginning, she'd fallen hard for Nash, and she'd loved him ever since. It was like breathing— it had come naturally to her.

But there was something fresh and exciting, something sweet and tender as a new bud on an old tree about the way she felt about him now. Their relationship had shifted into sharper focus, and, if possible, she'd fallen in love with him all over again.

She loved that boyish smile of his, the intelligence and wit, the goodness that was inherent in his character. He warmed her heart...and other significant parts of her as well, Zoe thought, as her lips curled into a private smile. Nash was a good man...who knew when to be a bad boy. And the things that he'd done to her last night were positively wicked. Remembered heat swirled below her navel and a tingly shiver contracted her nipples. Seeing his dark head feeding between her thighs had been the most erotic image Zoe had ever seen. Utterly incredible.

And she fully intended to reciprocate that sensual gesture tonight. Zoe belatedly wondered if he'd already gone to their room, but recalled him telling her he'd have to tend to a couple of things first.

He'd certainly taken his role as lodge owner very seriously, she thought, casting a glance around the cozy room. She'd seen him tend to guests with a warmth and sincerity that made her chest tighten, had watched him serve food, cut wood and even play fetch with that big black dog of George's.

And all the while he'd been looking out for her, had been trying to help her bring this criminal to justice. He'd been concerned for her welfare.

Zoe sighed contentedly. "You know what, Melanie? Nash is one helluva man."

Melanie's eyes twinkled and her lips slowly curled into a mysterious smile. "Indeed, he is."

Zoe reluctantly stood. "We should probably go to bed. We have a busy day tomorrow."

With a weary grunt, Melanie hoisted herself from the couch and absently set her empty cup on the coffee table. "You're right, of course. I'll see you in the morning."

Rather than leave the dirty cups in the great room for George or Nash to clean up, Zoe snagged both and decided to drop them off in the kitchen on the way to bed. Less work for someone, anyway.

But her steps slowed as she neared the closed door, because a fragment of conversation had reached her ears that sent her senses into the red zone.

"That's right," George was saying. "Colombia. Right. Well, they're the best, there's no doubt about that." He chuckled.

George? Zoe thought wildly. George was the culprit? Surely not, she scoffed. It had never occurred to her to do background checks or gather intel on the employees at the lodge. She'd been so certain that the thief was a member of the party. And yet, what else could he possibly be referring to, if not the diamonds?

"That's right. Naw, it's not a problem at all. I'm up, Louise. Just come on over and I'll sack 'em up for you. Come around back, though, so as not to wake the guests." There was a pause. "Sure," he laughed then, and for a moment it almost sounded as though he was flirting. "I'll share some with you."

Zoe didn't have any idea who this Louise person was, but she obviously worked for Boyle. Furthermore, George must be real confident in his place in the illegal organization, otherwise he'd never dream of skimming a little off the top. A thrill coursed through her. That meant she had more than a lackey within her sights, she had one of the bigger fishes in Boyle's nefarious pond.

George began whistling and she could hear him happily puttering around the kitchen. Arrogant bastard, Zoe thought, sickened that she'd actually grown fond of the cantankerous old coot.

Though her first inclination was to draw her weapon, burst through the door and nab him herself, she didn't. George appeared completely unconcerned, unhurried—hell, he was whistling, for pity's sake—which meant she had time to gather reinforcements.

Melanie was upstairs—too far away—so it had to be Nash. Zoe eased away from the door and made her way silently down the hall. She found him in their room.

"Nash," she said urgently. "Come on. I've found the thief and I have the son of a bitch cornered in the kitchen with the loot."

He blinked, gave her a blank look. "What?"

She grabbed his hand and yanked him along with her. "Thief, kitchen, loot," she whispered harshly, giving him the abbreviated version. She pulled her gun from her waistband. "Let's go."

He gulped when he saw the weapon, turned to dead weight when she wanted to hurry. "Do you need that, Zoe?"

"Let's hope not," she replied grimly. "That's why I brought you." Nash never carried a gun. His hands were lethal weapons, should have warning signs tattooed on them. Zoe was adept at self-defense, but she merely preferred the reassuring cold steel in her hand.

She dragged him onward and paused when she reached the kitchen, then did a button-your-lips gesture to Nash to make sure he didn't give away their position. She nudged the door open with her gun, peeked into the room. George stood at the counter, his back to her. Dammit, she didn't like that. Still, Louise would be here soon and then the odds of her doing this takedown smoothly greatly lessened.

It was now or never.

Gun drawn, Zoe exploded into the room, sending the door crashing against the wall. "Freeze!"

George jumped, screamed like a girl, and the

goods flew in every direction, scattering across the floor like marbles...dark marbles.

"George?" Nash said incredulously. "You think it's *George?"*

"The jig is up, George," Zoe said calmly, though her heart threatened to beat right out of her chest. She looked at the floor and at once recognized coffee beans, not the stolen jewels as she'd first suspected. "Where are the diamonds?"

George turned around, opened his mouth in outrage—about to deliver a load of brimstone for scaring him half to death, she imagined—then clamped it shut and paled when his gaze landed on the gun.

His watery gaze slid cautiously to Nash. "What do you plan to do about this, *Nash?"* George asked meaningfully, though the meaning was lost on her.

"Zoe, George is not the thief," Nash told her carefully, as though she were a bomb about to detonate. "I know that he's not the thief. You have to trust me on this. Put the gun away. Please."

Zoe's lips twisted. "I know you've grown rather fond of him, Nash, so his criminal activity is disheartening—I liked him, too. But I just overheard him on the phone. He has the diamonds, and a contact named Louise is presently on her way here to *share* them with George."

George's eyes widened, then he blushed. "Louise is a woman I...fancy," he said, seemingly embarrassed. "And she isn't coming over here for any blamed diamonds—she's coming over for coffee." He looked pointedly at the beans spilled on the counter and floor, then lifted his chin and stared mutinously at Zoe.

She heard Nash's breath leave in a sigh. "Louise is his girlfriend," he told her, his voice tired and strained. "And everyone on this side of the mountain gets coffee from George. It's a special blend from Colombia that his son sends him from overseas. He's a buyer for one of the larger coffee companies."

That neatly explained everything, but Zoe still wasn't quite convinced. "But how do we know that's all his son buys?"

George glared at her, then Nash. "How much longer are you going to let this fool business keep on?"

"George," Nash said warningly.

"Well, it's ridiculous," he snapped. "She's got a damn gun aimed at me and all I'm tryin' to do is make a little coffee for a friend."

"Zoe, George is not the thief," Nash repeated. A vein throbbed in his forehead. "*Put the gun away.*"

She hesitated. "Are you certain?"

He nodded fervently. "Yes."

She finally shrugged, then lowered the weapon and tucked it away. "I trust your judgment, Nash.

But if you're wrong, it's your ass on the line when it comes time to answer to Larson."

His shoulders slumped with relief. "I wouldn't have it any other way. But I'm not wrong."

"George, if I've wrongly accused you, then I am sorry," she told him, suitably contrite. Then she pinned him with a steely gaze. "However, if I find out that I'm right, and you are responsible, make no mistake, I will follow you to the ends of the earth if that's what it takes to hold you accountable."

Curiously, George looked more amused now than angry, when only seconds ago his livid countenance would have frightened little children. "I would expect nothing less, Ms. Wilder."

Bewildered by his abrupt change in attitude, Zoe nodded. "Good."

Nash passed a hand over his face. "Come on. I think we should go to bed." He nudged Zoe toward the door.

"Not so fast, buster," George said. A crafty gleam shone in his twinkling gaze. He nodded toward the floor. "I'm not cleanin' up this mess."

11

HE DIDN'T KNOW HOW MUCH more he could take, Lex thought tiredly. His nerves were stretched to the breaking point, and though he rarely took medication, he was seriously considering calling and asking Doc for a Xanax. A big one, too, the size of a freakin' horse pill.

When Faith had burst into his room like Suzy Homemaker meets Charlie's Angels, brandishing a gun and claiming to have found the thief, Lex had felt as if he'd stepped into an alternate reality.

And he had—*hers*.

Then, when he'd realized that she'd put George between the crosshairs, the bottom had dropped out of his stomach and his entire body had turned to lead.

George had been right. How much longer could this go on? When would her memory come back? And what would happen if it didn't?

Lex decided to go to the only other person who might have these concerns. He took the stairs two at a time, then found Trudy's door and knocked softly.

"Who is it?" she whispered.

"It's me. Open the door."

She flipped the lock, opened up, and he quickly ducked inside before anyone saw him. The last thing Zoe needed to think was that Nash was having an affair. He snorted, and realized that was really the least of his worries.

"What's wrong?"

Lex explained recent events, but rather than being suitably appalled—the appropriate response, considering Faith had almost shot his uncle, dammit—Trudy had the nerve to giggle.

His eyes widened in outrage. "I don't think—"

"I don't suppose now would be the right time to tell you that the gun's not real."

Astounded, Lex blinked. He gaped at her. "What?"

"It's not real. She picked it up at a spy shop before we left Nashville." Trudy's eyes glittered with mirth. "To my knowledge, she's never even held a weapon, m-much less learned how to f-fire one." Trudy attempted to smother a giggle with her fist, but failed miserably.

While it was comforting to know that the gun wasn't real, he would have probably found it considerably more comforting if he'd known it *before* she'd aimed it at his poor unsuspecting uncle.

Lex nonetheless felt a smile tease his lips. Now that it was over, he could see the humor in the situation. *Faith bursting into the room confident that she'd caught her thief, his uncle squealing like a stuck pig and the coffee beans flying through the air.* It was memorable, if nothing else.

"Look," Lex said, coming back to the point of his visit. "What happens tomorrow? What happens if she hasn't gotten her memory back before the book signing?"

Trudy winced regretfully. "We'll have to invent an emergency and leave." She shrugged. "That's all I know to do."

Lex nodded. He figured as much, but hearing the decision from Trudy made a hollow sensation expand in his chest.

She'd be gone, most likely forever.

"Are you all right?" Trudy asked.

"Yeah," Lex said distractedly. He rubbed the back of his neck. "I'd better get back downstairs. She'll miss me."

"That she will," Trudy replied, yet the innocuous comment seemed to hold some sort of double meaning, one that he didn't readily perceive.

That hollow ache in his chest spread like a cancer

and, by the time he reached his bedroom door, he felt utterly empty—numb—inside. The idea of her leaving chilled him to his very toes.

Lex let himself into their room...and the chilled sensation abruptly fled.

Faith stood when he entered the room, then lazily shrugged out of her gown and let the red fabric puddle to the floor in a silky hiss. Backlit by only the bedside lamp, her bare skin gleamed a creamy gold, and a halo of butterscotch curls framed her face and spilled over her shoulders, fell just short of her proud, upturned breasts. His gaze skimmed over her slim belly, that barely there waist, and every bit of moisture evaporated from his mouth as he took in the small nest of golden curls between her thighs. Snakes of heat writhed in his belly and his dick strained toward her like a divining rod.

"No interruptions tonight," she told him. "Take off your clothes."

God, yes, Lex thought. Who needed a nerve pill when an orgasm was imminent? He couldn't think of a better stress reliever.

He pushed every uncertainty, every worry, every care to the back of his brain. He'd deal with the whole sordid mess tomorrow.

Tonight, though she didn't know it, she was his. *No more lies,* Lex reminded himself as he slipped the buttons from their closures. From this moment on, every fraction of every second was the truth.

ZOE WATCHED A SERIES of emotions pass across Nash's face, and couldn't have named a single one save the last.

The last she recognized all too well, and the knowledge sent a triumphant thrill coursing through her because it was a heady mix of determination and desire. His ice-blue eyes bored into her, emanating heat like a blue flame, and that unwavering gaze kept her rooted to the floor, mesmerized by the intensity of attraction she saw there.

He systematically unbuttoned his shirt, then shrugged out of it and let it drop unheeded to the floor. Then he turned and locked the door. The click resonated like a single gunshot in the silence of the room. Zoe swallowed as a thick, sluggish heat wound through her limbs. Her lids drooped as need, more desperate than she could have ever imagined, pooled in her belly.

He casually unsnapped the button on his jeans, but didn't bother unzipping them—something she found thrillingly sexy—then stalked toward her. Heat radiated from his body, drew her like a moth to a flame. Then, in a gesture at once sweet and provocative, he gently framed her face and lowered his mouth to hers. A hum of relief and pleasure eased past her lips and she sank against him.

The kiss began slow, reverent, but quickly morphed into a seductive onslaught that made every cell in her body simmer with want. Warmth pooled between her thighs, slickened her folds. A current of electricity crackled down her spine and settled in her sex, tripping a breaker in her brain that shut down all cognitive synapses. Which was just as well because she didn't want to think—instinctively knew analyzing would be her enemy.

Sensation, heat, need obliterated everything else, and for the first time in her life—and she knew this with a certainty that defied all logic—she felt womanly and wanted...uninhibited.

She slid her hands over his magnificent chest, warm and smooth as polished marble, eliciting a shiver from his heavily muscled frame that gave her a thrill of feminine power. Addictive, that, Zoe thought, and instantly craved more.

"God, you're so beautiful," Nash murmured against her neck. Gooseflesh pebbled her skin. He breathed deeply, as though savoring her scent. His hands were gentle yet insistent as they moved over her body, shaping her back, her hips and her ass. He pulled her tightly to him and a flash fire ignited where their bodies touched. Her breasts grew heavy with want. Her nipples pearled, the desperate peaks shamelessly begging for his attention—the merest brush of his fingers, or better still, a lave of his tongue, a suckle from his talented mouth.

As though he possessed a direct line to her thoughts, Nash lowered that dark head and anchored it at her breast, drawing the taut crown fully into his hot mouth. A startled moan escaped her, and she found herself suddenly unable to support her own weight. She shifted until the backs of her legs touched the side of the bed, then brought him down with her.

The feel of his belly against hers, the delicious weight of his body made the fine hairs on her arms stand on end, pushed a groan of pure delight—of anticipation—from her lips.

His denim-clad legs brushed against hers and it dimly occurred to her that he was overdressed. She wanted to see him—all of him—and while being on the receiving end of his undivided attention was fantastic, Zoe didn't want to just be worshipped—she wanted to do a little worshipping herself. Wanted to make him sigh, moan, groan, whimper and beg. Wanted to feel every muscle grow rigid with need, to watch him grit his teeth and try to hold back, then succumb to the sensation and to give everything to her, leaving nothing in reserve. She wanted to watch those ice-blue eyes melt with satisfaction as he came.

Though it took every ounce of will she possessed, Zoe pulled his head away from her breast. "You're overdressed," she rasped, her voice rusty with want.

Those blue eyes suddenly twinkled and a slow, sexy grin slid over his firm, yet full, lips. "That's easily remedied."

He slid back, straightened, and lowered his zipper, then shucked his pants and briefs in one fell swoop that left her instantly amazed and incredibly...hungry.

She'd noted his size before. He was a tall man, built on an enormous scale, so reason would indicate that every part of him would be constructed in a proportionate manner.

But Nash possessed his portion and easily half of another, Zoe thought, her eyes glued to that mesmerizing, awe-inspiring part of his anatomy, and the idea that *that* would soon be driving in and out of her, pushing her to heights of unparalleled sexual ecstasy, made every particle in her body sing with depraved expectation.

Of their own volition, her hands reached out and touched him, pulling a startled hiss from between his teeth. "Damn," he croaked. His thighs shook, then went rigid.

Zoe shaped both hands around him, reveled in the novelty of the sheer size and heat, the soft-as-silk skin, the tension vibrating beneath her palms. She worked her hands back and forth, slid a finger over the rosy tip and caught a single pearl of desire that she'd milked from him.

She wanted more.

She looked up, caught his gaze, then purposely inserted her finger into her mouth and slowly sucked it clean.

Nash swallowed convulsively and a strangled bark of laughter burst from his throat. "You're going to be the death of me, you know that?"

"Yeah, well, do me a favor and don't die until I'm through with you, okay?" Zoe replied with a chuckle. Then she took him into her mouth, and the taste of him, the sheer masculine flavor, saturated her tongue, stirred her senses, pulling a moan of pure delight from the back of her throat.

Lex gritted his teeth and his head fell back. He tunneled his fingers into her hair, massaged her scalp. It was like trying the first bite of a succulent dessert, then discovering that you loved the taste, Zoe thought.

178 *Unforgettable*

She'd sampled, she'd liked, now she would happily clean her plate.

She scooted closer, then pulled him as far into her mouth as she could, curled her tongue around him in slow, thorough strokes, licking him as though he were a melting ice cream cone.

Nash's breathing grew rapid, evidence of his pleasure, and those manly nonsensical sounds were her reward, fed the fever burning brightly inside her. Her sex throbbed, wept, and that achy hollow place inside her begged to be filled, pushed away and obliterated until she didn't know where she ended and he began. Her body craved release, was utterly desperate for it. These thoughts and needs flittered through her head, and she used them to draw reaction from him. She sucked, she licked, she nibbled, she stroked, desperate to make him as crazy as she was, to make him want her as much as she did him.

She could feel the tension building within him, could feel it hum against her mouth, could taste the salty essence that preceded climax, and knew that with another clever flick and suckle, she could make him explode.

He seemed to realize this as well, because he growled a miserable sort of howl, then drew back away from her hungry ministrations.

"Not this way," he panted. His fevered gaze tangled with hers and another hot thrill whipped through her.

She'd done that.

She'd made him mindless with need.

"I want to be inside you," he told her, his voice a harsh rasp. He squeezed his eyes tightly shut. "I *need* to be inside you."

Zoe raked her nails lightly down his chest and her gaze searched his. "I can't wait for you to be inside me." Desire made her voice so low and sultry she barely recognized it as her own.

Nash bent and retrieved a condom from the nightstand. He tore the packet open, then swiftly withdrew the protection and, hands shaking slightly, smoothed it into place. Then he joined her on the bed. When he would have positioned himself once more between her thighs, Zoe rolled him onto his back and straddled him. Her wet sex rode the ridge of his arousal. She blew out a shaky breath at the contact, felt her lids flutter shut as the sensation washed through her.

His eyes widened slightly, then another melting grin curved his lips. "Want the dominant position, do you?"

"No." She bent and flicked her tongue over his ruddy nipple. Smoothed her hands over the intriguing planes of his chest. Sheer perfection. All hers. "I just don't want to risk bad luck," she murmured, momentarily distracted by the jerk of his penis against her nether folds. Her breath caught. "The last time we tried it your way, we were interrupted."

He smiled knowingly and a tortured laugh stuttered out of his lungs. "Baby, the house could blow down around me, and I promise, I'm not going anywhere."

His gaze drifted over her breasts, down her belly and settled where their sexes met. He licked his lips, then arched up and took her breast into his mouth. Fire stirred in her loins and she ground her hips against him to smother it, but the futile act only fanned the flames, intensified the heat.

She whimpered. Nash coupled the suckling with a deliberate slide between her slickened folds, snatching the breath from her lungs. He cupped her other breast, tweaked the nipple and nudged once more, this time bumping her clit. She whimpered, let her head drop back as she moved back and forth along the enormous length of him until the prelude simply wasn't enough. She had to have him inside her—*now.*

She tilted her hips, took him in hand and guided him to her entrance, then slowly—*oh, God, so very slowly*, because she wanted to savor every inch, every ridge and vein, wanted to feel it all—lowered herself onto his throbbing shaft.

Nash's neck arched back, revealing vulnerability and corded vein. His hands gripped her hips and every muscle in his body went rigid. The picture was indelibly imprinted on her brain—she'd never forget it. Never. A tendril of memory, of some distant yet significant thought, teased her once more, but Zoe didn't even try to draw it near. She was too consumed by the feel of him buried inside her so deeply, so perfectly she wanted to weep. That sensation made everything else fade into insignificance. There was no past, no future, only the present.

Nash flexed his hips beneath her, pushed up and withdrew, creating a delicious drag between their joined bodies. Zoe winced as the pleasure barbed through her. She lifted and sank, lifted and sank, purposely and purposefully until the desire to drag the ecstasy out was forgotten and nothing but the race for release mattered.

Nash sensed her change in demeanor and responded with urgent enthusiasm that made her breasts jiggle on her chest as she absorbed the force of his thrusts. She rode him while he heaved beneath her, their rhythm instinctively in sync. He reached down between their joined bodies and massaged the sensitive nub hidden in her drenched curls.

Starbursts flared behind her lids. She felt the first flash of beginning climax tug sharply in her womb, and breathing raggedly, she upped the tempo. "Oh, God," she cried, tormented by the exquisite tension. "Oh, please." She winced, whimpered.

It was— She couldn't—

Nash thumbed her harder and her world shattered. The climax broke over her. Her mouth opened in a soundless scream, and she couldn't have lifted her lids if her life had depended upon it. She tensed as she surfed the pleasure, then melted against his chest as the last tremors subsided.

Zoe didn't move, couldn't, wouldn't. She loved the feel of him inside her, cherished the most intimate connection. Nash's breathing finally returned to a normal rhythm and his large warm hands slid over her back in a soothing fashion. He probed the indentation of her spine, doodled around the dimples at the small of her back.

"Mmm. That was incredible," she murmured against his chest.

He didn't reply, seemed lost in his own thoughts, then finally lifted her head and made her look into his eyes. "I need you to remember something. It's very important, okay?"

Emotion churned those ice-blue eyes to a stormy hue. "Sure," she said, perplexed. "What is it?"

"I'm in with love you."

Something warm tingled in her chest and a smile curved her mouth. "I—"

"I've been in love with you since the first moment I saw you," he continued, his voice curiously intense, as though it was vitally important that she understood him. "I think that you are the most remarkable woman I have ever met. I look at you and I..." He looked away, as though unable to find the right words, then that tormented gaze met hers again. "I look at you and I melt. Something happens to me in here." He thumped his chest. "I just need you to know it. I need you to remember it."

Now this was a completely new side of her bad-ass, Zoe thought, unaccountably touched. It was soft and approachable, vulnerable and all too real. Her eyes misted with emotion and she kissed his cheek. She could barely speak over the lump in her throat. "Oh, Nash. I love you, too."

His hands had resumed their mesmerizing massage, but stilled when she spoke, and his chest deflated with a small sigh. But before she could pon-

der the unusual reaction, he suddenly framed her
face once more and kissed her so deeply, so thoroughly, it drove everything save him out of her
mind.

12

LEX CAREFULLY—regretfully—disentangled himself from Faith's sleeping form. Though he hadn't set the clock last night—he'd been too busy making love—his internal alarm had nonetheless gone off shortly after dawn this morning. Sleeping in was a luxury those in his profession simply didn't enjoy. Guests needed to check out, to have their luggage brought down. They needed breakfast, coffee, directions. Lex sighed. Always something. No matter how much he wanted to linger in bed with his lover, it simply wasn't an option.

His lover.

Lex mentally reviewed every single second of last night. Soft sighs, little mewls, wicked groans of pleasure, the feel of him plunging in and out of her tight heat...and hard, earth-shattering, soul-shaping orgasms. Contentment sprang inside him from some hidden well previously unplumbed.

His gaze drifted over her woefully familiar face, the smooth brow, sloping curve of her cheek, the small yet determined chin, those lush, plum-soft lips. A band tightened around his chest, momentarily preventing him from drawing a breath.

God, she was perfect. Utterly, completely perfect, and though he knew that today was the last day he would share with her, though he knew that she'd leave—and at some point remember her identity and the part he'd played in this weekend—though he knew she'd feel betrayed, he couldn't for the life of him change a single thing that had happened last night.

Even when she'd unwittingly broken his heart.

I love you, too, Nash.

And she did. She loved Nash Austin. She didn't love him, and no matter how hard he'd tried to make her see *him*—make her see Lex Ellenburg—she hadn't.

Last night she'd made love to her fantasy hero—one she'd created, for pity's sake—and he'd made love to the woman he wanted to spend the rest of his life with. A bitter smile shaped his lips. Appropriate punishment, he supposed, for going along with this ill-conceived farce.

Lex didn't care what Trudy said, how well she thought she knew her friend. Faith would feel betrayed. He had tried to soften the damage by pouring out his heart to her last night—it had been imperative that she understood, that she didn't doubt how he felt about her. She would doubt, he knew, but hopefully there would be just enough sincerity behind the memory to make way for forgiveness.

That's what he was banking on, the only thing that kept him from absolutely losing his mind.

Today she would leave—he supposed Trudy would have Larson fake a call and send Nash to some remote outpost of civilization until her memory came back—and Lex didn't have any way to prevent that from happening.

Furthermore, though the time would come, he didn't know what sort of apology he could offer for making love to her, knowing that she thought he was someone else. What penance could be paid to make something like that right?

Whatever it was, he'd gladly pay it. Yes, she would leave here today, and a little part of him would leave right along with her, but when her memory returned, he would follow her to the ends of the earth if need be to make her come back.

He wanted to go to bed with her each night and wake up with her in the morning. He wanted her to burn meals in his kitchen, accidentally ruin his favorite shirt, hold his hand during an afternoon walk. He wanted her to scream at him when he was foolish, praise him for small victories and comfort him when he grieved. He wanted to watch her belly swell with his child, to wipe her brow when she gave birth. He wanted to make love to her on rainy days, on the braided rug in front of the fireplace. He wanted to surprise her with gifts, to be her friend and confidant, her partner.

In short, he wanted to spend his life with her. Everything. The good, the bad and the ugly. It didn't matter, so long as she was with him.

A smile tinged his lips. Didn't want much, did he?

The trick would be making her want it as much, showing her that while her fictional hero might be able to kick ass across every continent, he couldn't love her back.

Lex could, and would, given the opportunity.

ZOE SHIFTED, but didn't open her eyes. She'd been having the most delicious dream. She and Nash had made love all night, and he'd told her that he loved her, and then he'd put his money where his mouth was by making sure that she believed it.

He hadn't just made love to her—he'd worshipped her.

He'd washed kisses all over her body, he'd inspected every inch of her, measured each part with his mouth and hands. He'd pumped in and out of her, punctuating each powerful thrust with an *I* then *love* then *you* until she'd laughed and then cried, because she'd felt her foolish heart begin to soften and truly believe him. His love felt real now, not just assumed or taken for granted. He'd chiseled it into her heart, much as a sculptor hammered away at the piece of stone. He hadn't stopped until he'd been certain that she believed him.

In the wee hours of the morning, when he'd wrung the last ounce of energy from her listless, totally satiated body, he'd rolled her with him onto her side, then pressed a reverent kiss to her temple, and murmured, "Please remember."

She'd drifted off to sleep, cocooned in the warmth and happiness of knowing that she was loved without reservation, without reason, and completely without condition.

She slid a hand over to Nash's side of the bed and frowned when she found it empty.

She'd woken up alone....

The noise from the shower suddenly drifted toward her, accounting for her lonely state. She glanced at the clock and winced. She should probably take a shower as well, Zoe thought with a pang of regret. She'd really rather stay in bed, then have Nash join her in it when he came out. But the *To Catch a Thief* party concluded this morning, so she really couldn't spare the time.

Which reminded her. She'd need to get together with Melanie and see if Larson had turned up any possible leads on the true thief. She was honestly at a loss. Didn't know what to do. It was beginning to look as if she'd have her first unsuccessful mission, and the idea galled her to no end. She'd had a perfect record, and some two-bit thief was going to ruin it.

Damn.

She simply couldn't let that happen. The bastard was here, and she'd catch him. She had to.

But first she had to have a shower. A vision of Nash's naked form suddenly loomed to life in her mind and her insides instantly simmered with warmth. Perhaps a little multitasking was in order, Zoe thought, as a wicked grin slid across her lips. If she wanted sex and needed a shower, then if she simply joined Nash, she could have both.

She opened the bedside drawer for the necessary protection and was just about to slide it shut when a flash of poison green caught her attention.

A funny feeling inexplicably camped in her neck.

Zoe stilled. It was a book, she realized, one that, for reasons that escaped her, seemed oddly familiar. Her insides knotted with anxiety and her hands shook, and she seemed to have forgotten how to breathe. The title—*Murder and Mayhem*—drew her attention, but it was the author's name that made her heart pound in her chest, made her mouth grow parched. Made a wild buzzing noise blare through her head.

Faith Bonner.

She didn't know what made her do it, where the notion came from or what intuitive little voice whispered the command, but she turned the book over...

...and stared at her own reflection.

A picture of herself smiled up from the back jacket.

The anxiety in her gut continued to twist mercilessly, her hands trembled violently and a band of tension tightened around her head. Then the buzzing abruptly stopped, followed by a rapid-fire stream of images and sounds, ideas and perceptions, truths and lies, the last of which made a sob form in the back of her throat.

Oh, God. The impact of what this meant struck her hard, like a simultaneous blow to the head and a dropkick to the gut. It had been lies. All lies. A part he'd played...

I'm in love with you. Please remember.

She remembered all right. Everything. Every sordid detail. Humiliation and regret burned through her, followed immediately by a pain so intense she could barely keep from doubling over, so intense tears wouldn't come and would never suffice, would never wash away the hurt.

You're beautiful. I'm in love with you. I look at you and I melt.

He'd been playing the part of Nash, Faith realized, utterly wretched, and he'd done it quite well. Everyone had been playing a part, Trudy included. Somehow they'd convinced the guests to play along, as well. Trudy, Faith was sure, had gone along with the ruse because of the professional and financial aspects that ultimately had to be considered. As Faith's assistant, she had to look out for her boss's best interests. The guests had played along because they didn't know any better.

The question was, what had propelled Lex Ellenburg to play along?

He chose that moment to come out of the bathroom. He was completely naked. Little droplets of water clung to his shoulders and chest, and his hair was slicked back from his forehead. She fought the need that instantly bombarded her, focused on the hurt instead, though it was hard. So much harder than it had any right to be.

"Ah. You're up." He smiled at her and for a moment she believed the warmth and affection she saw shining in that too gorgeous, cruelly deceptive gaze. Then that gaze dropped to the book in her hand. He stilled and the smile slowly faded. He looked back at her once more and the gaze was shuttered this time, as though a shadow had moved into place to hide his emotions.

"Why did you do it?" she asked, and congratulated herself for sounding somewhat normal, considering she felt like one of those cartoon characters that had been blown to smithereens by a truckload of TNT, but didn't readily fall apart.

His shoulders slumped, then he hurriedly secured around his hips the towel he'd been drying his hair with.

Faith smirked. "Little late for propriety, wouldn't you say?"

She, too, was naked, but she refused to cover herself. There hadn't been a single part of her this man hadn't intimately acquainted himself with. She'd obviously been suffering from some sort of crazy delusion or amnesia. That she clearly hadn't realized what she'd been doing was the only comfort she could call her own out of this damn charade.

He flushed guiltily. "Faith—"

"Why did you do it?" she repeated. She didn't know why it mattered, but it did.

It mattered *a lot*.

He frowned. "Do you remember going to Doc Givens?"

Her lips twisted. "I remember everything."

He shot her a look. "Er...okay. Doc met with Trudy and me in the hallway while you were getting dressed. He told us that you had amnesia."

"From the blow to the head?" Faith asked skeptically. It had only been a scratch. Nothing that should have put her into that sort of state.

He winced. "Not exactly. He said that the blow was most likely the catalyst from your subconscious that had propelled the switch. You'd been preparing for the role, you knew the character as well as yourself, that Zoe was most likely merely an extension of you."

Faith rolled her eyes. "Hardly."

He looked up at her. "I've read the books and I see many similarities. At any rate, he said to play along, that you would come back when you were ready. So that's what we did." He shrugged lightly, but then his gaze drifted off, no longer able to hold hers. And, in that instant, she knew. Faith fought down the nausea clawing the back of her throat.

She closed her eyes. Opened them. "She's paying you, isn't she?"

"She offered a bonus, yes," he finally admitted. "But you don't understand—"

Faith snorted bitterly. "Oh, I understand. How much?" Though every instinct told her to flee, Faith couldn't until she knew precisely how much of her hard-earned money had gone to this man to sleep with her.

"Look. It's not as simple as it sounds. You have to listen to me—"

"How much?"

A beat slid to three before he reluctantly told her. She whistled low. No wonder he'd done such a good job playing his part, Faith thought bitterly. She could have hired an entire host of men and had a weeklong orgy in Greece for that price. She bit her lip and cursed the moisture that pricked her lids.

She would not cry.

She wouldn't cry over this opportunistic son of a bitch.

"Oh, Christ," Lex swore. "I knew you would feel this way. I tried to tell Trudy, but she wouldn't listen. I don't give a damn about the money. Keep it. I don't care."

He dropped to his knees before her and tried to take her hand, but Faith jerked away to avoid the touch. He looked as though she'd slapped him, but considering his extensive acting skills, she didn't trust the sentiment. "Don't touch me," she said, in a voice so low and hard she didn't recognize it as her own. "Don't ever touch me again." She enunciated each word with careful deliberation.

"Do you remember what I told you last night?"

She looked away. "I've already told you that I remember everything."

"Then you have to remember that I love you." A desperate, quiet urgency laced his voice and it rang with sincerity. But it couldn't be true. It couldn't. Even if he did fancy himself in love with someone, it wasn't her—it was Zoe.

She shattered inside.

"Please, Faith," he implored. "I told you it was important that you remembered. Please," he whispered softly.

From the corner of her eye, she let her gaze linger on the familiar planes of his face, those firm lips, pale blue eyes, the scar at his temple. So like Nash...but not, she realized, and the most horrible, awful, heart-wrenching thing occurred to her.

She'd fallen in love with the bastard.

"I love you," he repeated, his haunted gaze glued to her profile.

Though it hurt more than she could have ever imagined, Faith finally forced herself to look at him. Her eyes watered. "No you don't, Mr. Ellenburg," she said, her mouth curving into a sad smile. "You love a character I've been playing. Now if you'll excuse me, I think I should find Trudy and finish up this *To Catch a Thief* event."

"I'm not in love with a damn character," he retorted hotly. "I'm in love with *you*."

Faith stood and, with as much dignity as she could muster, put on her robe. She could feel little pieces of her heart breaking in her chest, sharp, jagged chunks that tore at her emotions. "I know I should probably tell you that I appreciate everything you've done to make this run smoothly, but I hope you'll understand if I'm not up to the required pleasantries. I'll let Trudy take care of that."

"Dammit, Faith." He shoved a hand through his hair. "Please listen to me. *Don't do this.*"

She belatedly noticed her clothes and toiletries littered about the room. "I'll have Trudy collect my things, as well."

Then, without a backward glance, and though she had to force herself to move, she let herself out of the room.

Out of his life.

The house was silent, utterly quiet, and she needed a place to grieve alone, at least for a few minutes. She needed time to regroup. To put herself back together before she had to face Trudy or anybody else. A sob wrenched out of her throat, quickly followed by a wave of nausea so strong she hurried into the kitchen and retched into the sink. She'd just finished wiping her mouth when she realized that she wasn't alone.

Faith slowly straightened and turned around.

The Millers stood frozen, Mrs. Miller at the fridge and Mr. Miller at the counter. It took a full five seconds to absorb what she saw, and yet she still couldn't make sense of it. Mrs. Miller had been in the act of pouring one box of salt into the milk, and from the looks of things, Mr. Miller had been contaminating the sugar and flour canisters with the other one.

"What the hell are you doing?" Faith demanded. Why would they—

"Nothing," Mrs. Miller said guiltily. "We're, uh... We're going to fix breakfast."

"Right," Mr. Miller confirmed. The man was an abysmal liar.

Faith quickly dialed through her fractured memory and tried to recall what else she'd seen in their room—other than the S&M toys—and instantly remembered the many photos of the lodge, the notes about square footage. A frown wrinkled her brow, and though she had absolutely no desire to see Lex again, she knew she had to let him know about this. Something was up. She had a strong suspicion—

her gaze bounced between the two guilty looking faces—but she'd need to see what he thought.

Rather than risk leaving them alone, she walked to the door and bellowed down the hall for him. Seconds later, he rushed into the kitchen—and drew up short at the scene that greeted him. He looked at her, then to the Millers. The salt registered and she watched comprehension dawn on his woefully familiar face. Pain clogged her throat, swelled in her chest.

"What's going on here?" he asked, disbelief still edging out the anger she knew would come. "Margie? James?"

"They were pouring the salt I found in their briefcase into your milk, sugar and flour. They're sabotaging you," Faith told him, her tone flat and emotionless. Would that she could feel that way, as well. "They're regulars, right?"

He nodded, his face a thunderstruck mask. A flash of pity for him surfaced, but she ruthlessly beat it down.

"Now wait just a minute," Margie exclaimed. "It's not—"

Faith shot her a glance that quelled the rest of what Margie had intended to say. "Then I imagine that they've been doing it all along. You might want to go back and cross-reference any repairs you've had to make with their visits." She paused. "It hadn't seemed important at the time, but they also have many pictures of the lodge, along with notes about square footage and other facts about your place in that briefcase."

Lex's gaze swung from her to them. His face was a pale mask of hurt and anger. "My central AC unit. My computer." His eyes widened. "Those goddamn bugs!"

James and Margie ducked their heads, unable to meet his gaze. "It wouldn't have come to this if you'd just taken our offer," Margie finally said. "It was a generous one. You'd have been better off."

He laughed bitterly. "My God. I never suspected— I never thought— And it was you all along. Hell, no wonder I couldn't get ahead, no wonder things kept going wrong. You almost ruined me!" he exclaimed. He passed a hand over his face, tried to pull himself together and after several minutes seemed to have calmed down enough to speak. "I'll have George total the repair bills and I'll expect a check before you leave—which you will be doing as swiftly as you can get your shit together—otherwise, I'll call the sheriff and this will really get nasty."

Margie paled, then nodded, and she and her

husband exited the room. Once they'd left, Lex turned to face Faith. He swallowed. "Thank you."

Her throat burned. "You're welcome." She turned to go.

"Faith." Her step faltered and her breath hitched.

"I wasn't lying when I said I loved you."

"I never thought you were, Lex." That was the part that hurt the worst. She bit her lip in a futile effort to stem the tears stinging her eyes. A sadness so profound and so deep cut through her it almost sent her back to the sink. "You're just in love with the wrong woman."

She turned once more and walked away, and this time, thankfully, he didn't try to stop her.

13

"I'M VERY SORRY," Trudy said with a melancholy smile. "I thought I was helping both of you. I'd seen the way you looked at each other and I thought it wouldn't hurt to give nature a nudge...." She shrugged wearily. "She'll change her mind. Just give it a few days."

Lex and Trudy stood on the porch, while Faith had gone ahead to the SUV. She'd abandoned her Zoe-wear and had once again dressed in a comfy camel-colored sweater and matching pants. Her lips were painted a soft raspberry, not the bright red she'd worn all weekend. She'd twisted her hair up on top of her head and anchored it with a clip of some sort, revealing the delicate skin at her nape. Need and affection broadsided him. She was soft and womanly...gorgeous, and he wanted her so desperately that he ached from the inside out.

He watched her bend down and pet Beano, and he managed a faint smile. At least she'd gotten over her fear of dogs.

The finale of the *To Catch a Thief* event had been

a smashing success. The guests had been so thrilled with the way it had turned out that they hadn't noticed their star wore a strained smile, or that her pale brown eyes had darkened with pain. She'd finished out the role of Zoe, then shared a brunch and signed books. She'd done it all without complaint, but he knew that she felt every bit as devastated as he did.

When they'd stood in front of the crowd and taken their bows, he'd felt her tense the moment he'd moved into place beside her. He'd wanted to reach for her, bring her back to him. But he'd known she wouldn't welcome a touch from him, so he'd fisted his hands at his sides, and smiled because he'd had to, and all the while, he'd been frozen inside. Numb. Hollow.

"It'll be all right," Trudy told him. "You'll see. She just needs time," she repeated, as though saying it over and over would make it true. Trudy reached into her purse and handed him a check.

Lex took it and tore it in half, then handed it back to her. He hadn't been lying when he'd said she could keep the money. He'd manage somehow. He always did. And it should be considerably easier now that the Millers weren't trying to ruin him. He had Faith to thank for that, as well. He still couldn't believe it, couldn't believe they'd been so duplicitous, sneaky and underhanded.

Trudy gave him a sympathetic smile. "I knew you'd do that, so I gave another check to George, who has promised to deposit it." She looked around, inspected the premises with a fond yet critical eye. "It's a beautiful place...but it could use a new roof, and I hear you've had a bad year." She descended the steps. "Thanks, Lex. For everything."

Trudy joined Faith by the SUV and a mere thirty seconds later, they were gone.

His entire world suddenly dimmed around him, faded into colorless insignificance. A lump formed in his throat, but rather than succumb to the emotion, he forced it aside with anger and self-recriminations. Then, when he felt somewhat steadier, he hammered that cold hard fury into determination.

He would not lose her.

He would not.

He'd wait a few days, as Trudy had suggested. Then he was going to give Faith Bonner the hero she wanted...or die trying.

"I WANT THAT ONE," Faith said.

The clerk at the animal shelter looked at her as if

she'd lost her mind. "You sure? We've got some adorable puppies right over here."

Faith shook her head. "No." She smiled. "I'll take that one."

That one was probably the saddest excuse for a dog that had ever walked the planet. He was old and scrawny, with patches of fur missing, and he'd lost part of his right ear. He was a mismatch of color, reminded her of the old shag carpet she'd once had in her bedroom.

But his eyes were kind and weary, and he looked as if he needed her love more than any of the other animals in here. The puppies would be adopted— they were adorable, after all—but this guy was a hairsbreadth from being euthanized.

She wanted him.

They were a perfect match.

In short order, Faith loaded up her new friend into the front seat of her car, then, praying that he wouldn't puke on her upholstery, she drove to one of the pet-friendly stores where she could take her new animal inside to shop with her.

A couple of women with cute little toy breeds shot her pitying glances when they saw her ugly dog, but she determinedly ignored them. Her dog had character, mileage, which made up for cute. She'd decided to name him Roy. For some reason, the plain old-fashioned moniker suited him. She loaded her cart with dog food, a dog bed, toys— she doubted he'd play with them, but she wanted him to have them, anyway—and a couple of raw-hide bones, then breezed through the checkout and, loaded down, aimed her car toward home.

She patted Roy's head. "You're going to like it here, Roy," she told him, amazed at how natural talking to the animal felt. "It's comfy and you'll have a backyard you can play in."

A vision of Lex's woods flashed through her mind, and she couldn't help but admit that he'd probably like it better at Oak Crest. She could see his lazy hide lounging on the back porch there. Ir-ritated, Faith shook herself.

Honestly, ever since she'd gotten home, she'd constantly compared her stately colonial to the worn but homey look of the lodge. Her bright white rooms, the brick fireplace, the Italian marble floors. Things that she'd once loved about her house no longer gleamed as nicely as they had be-fore. She missed the warm cozy feeling of the lodge, the whisper of wind in the trees, the crisp clean air. Faith sighed.

But mostly she missed Lex.

All the way home, Trudy had repeatedly ex-plained what had happened, had tried to make her see reason. Had told her everything George had shared about Lex's family history and financial situation. No wonder the place had felt so homey—it had been home to three generations of Ellenburgs. Love, loss and life breathed from every timber holding the place together, oozed from the very walls. Faith had been enchanted from the first moment she'd seen it, could feel that familial tug drawing her in.

But she realized now it had been Lex she'd been drawn to. He'd put every bit of himself into that place and she'd felt that presence the minute she'd gotten out of the car. She'd been doomed to love him before she'd ever laid eyes on him.

It was funny, Faith thought. All this time she'd thought she knew what made a good hero, what made a man a woman's dream come true. But she didn't know anything. Lex couldn't speak seven different languages. He couldn't deactivate a bomb, or kill a man in sixteen different ways in less than thirty seconds. He didn't know how to fly a plane, or any of those other things she'd had Nash Austin do over the years.

Lex was just a good man, with a good heart. He was loyal and, despite what had happened over the weekend, she knew he was honest. He cared for his uncle George, he provided jobs for people who needed them in a depressed economy, probably to his own detriment, and he wasn't opposed to washing dishes when the need arose.

He was a hero, Faith had realized. Lex Ellenburg was the hero of her heart.

And he was in love with another woman—Zoe Wilder. But she could hardly fault him for that, now could she? Millions of readers had fallen in love with her kick-ass heroine. Faith loved her. How could she be angry with him for falling for Zoe, when so many had done the same? She couldn't.

So she'd wept. She'd wept for a life that might have been. Wept for a thousand nights she'd never share with him, nights she'd never spend in the lodge. The children they'd never have. The love they'd never make again. And when she'd cried all the tears she could cry, she'd gone to the pound and gotten Roy. He wouldn't make the kind of partner Lex would, but at least she wouldn't be alone anymore. She'd have company, something to care for besides the hero and heroine in her story.

She'd have to start a new book soon, but where she normally felt a rush of anticipation at the beginning of a new story, Faith couldn't seem to work up any enthusiasm for it. She was jealous of Zoe and, though Nash and Lex were nothing alike, the physical similarity was there, along with the achingly sweet reminder of the past weekend.

Lex had told her to remember, had stressed how important that was. She did. She remembered being loved so thoroughly, so completely by the man she'd fallen in love with that her heart broke every time she called his image to mind.

Which was frequently.

She remembered being loved…as Zoe, but not Faith.

Faith slowed as she neared her driveway. An older model pickup truck sat in her drive. She eased in beside it, then panic set in when she realized a man sat in the cab. She didn't have to see him to know that it was Lex. Every hair stood on end and her nape prickled with awareness. Her stomach dropped to her toes and a tingle raced down her spine. What was he— How did— Her eyes narrowed.

Trudy.

Lex got out of the truck when he saw her. A dark bruise stained the left side of his cheek and a cut split his bottom lip. Two fingers were splinted and wrapped with white medical tape. He winced as his feet hit the pavement.

Panic set in. What the hell? "What happened to you?"

"I'll explain in a minute." He looked into the front seat of her car and a familiar smile spread across his handsome face. He leaned against the window. "What have you got in there?"

Bewildered, Faith stared at him. "That's Roy."

His grin widened. "Roy?"

"No special meaning. I just liked it."

"I do, too. It suits him."

"I just got him," Faith said. "We're still getting acquainted."

He nodded, then his gaze shifted to the back seat. He smacked a hand against the hood of her car. "Let me help you get these things inside."

Before she could form a protest, he'd gathered the boxes from the back seat, leaving her to follow with the dog.

Faith scrambled to snap the leash onto his collar, then found her keys and met Lex at the door.

"Nice place."

Not compared to his, Faith thought. After being in his home, hers felt...sterile. But she thanked him anyway, then ushered him inside.

"Where do you want his food station?"

On your back porch. What the hell was he doing here? Didn't he have any idea how painful this was for her? How humiliating? "Er...next to the fridge will be fine."

Lex efficiently set things up, filled Roy's food and water dishes, before he finally stood. He crossed his arms over his chest and leaned against her counter. "He's a good dog. He has character."

Her eyes widened slightly and a reluctant smile slid across her lips. "I thought so, too." Her gaze drifted over Lex's battered face once more. "Now do you want to tell me what happened to you? What? Did Pooh play too rough?"

Lex grinned. "No, nothing like that."

"Then what?"

"I got beat up in Hero class."

"What?"

"I got beat up in Hero class," he repeated, to her absolute astonishment. "If you want a hero, then I'll be a hero. I'm taking karate—and getting my ass kicked by a dozen eight-year-olds every day, I might add—and I've signed up for a couple of foreign language classes at the local community college. The bomb thing is going to be a little tricky. Curiously, you can find all sorts of Web sites on how to build them, but hardly any on how to de-activate one." He grimaced. "Flying lessons are a little out of my price range right now, but I'm working on it."

Faith shook her head. *Hero class.* Karate and foreign languages, bombs and flying lessons? What on earth?

Lex moved toward her and before she knew what he was about, he reverently traced a path down the side of her face. "Let me be your hero, Faith," he said softly. "I'll do whatever it takes, whatever you want me to do." Those ice-blue eyes searched hers. "I love you, remember?"

She swallowed tightly, fought the overwhelming urge to believe him, to sink against him. "You love Zoe, not me."

He shook his head, brushed a lock of hair from her brow. "Zoe's a great heroine, a fantastic character. She's entertaining...but she's not you. I fell in love with *you* the moment I saw you and I've been in love with you ever since. She's a character," he repeated. "And a good one, no doubt. But she's not you." He paused. "Any more than I'm Nash. But for you, I'll try to be. I'll be whoever you want me to be, so long as I can be yours."

Faith stilled as what he was saying finally took hold in her whirling brain. He loved her...and was willing to turn himself into a badass like Nash because that's what he thought she wanted. But she didn't want that. She wanted him. Just him.

She moistened her lips and lifted her gaze to his. "I don't want you to be anyone but yourself. You're right—Zoe and Nash are characters, but they're not real. Until I met you, I thought I knew what made a hero...but I didn't. Being able to speak different languages, learning karate, flying a plane. Those are not the characteristics of my hero," Faith told him.

A hopeful glint lit his gaze and he sidled closer. "What are the characteristics of your hero?" he murmured, his voice deep and rough with longing.

She looped her arms around his neck. "Oh, he's tall, dark and handsome. He's honest and loyal, intelligent and funny." She peeked at him beneath lowered lashes. "And he's sexy as hell."

Lex's warm hands settled at her waist. "Oh? What else?"

A grin played at her lips. "He's not much of a fighter—I hear little kids have been beating him up. But he's got the heart of a lion...and he owns a little lodge up in the mountains that I absolutely love."

His eyes twinkled. "He sounds like a great guy."

"He can be a little arrogant at times," she admonished playfully. She paused, her gaze tangled with his. "But I love him, anyway."

Lex stilled. "You do?"

Faith felt a smile slide across her lips. "I do."

He kissed her then, long and deep, until her

knees weakened and desire pooled in her loins, and nothing but a bright future lay spread out before them. Breathing hard, he finally tore his mouth from hers. "I love you, too…remember?"

She most certainly did—and she would never forget.

Epilogue

"YOU NEED TO COME inside," Lex admonished softly. He bent and brushed a kiss over Faith's cheek, rubbed a hand over her rounded belly. "Mothers-to-be have to stay warm, and I know a really good way to heat you up fast," he murmured suggestively.

"I'm almost finished with this scene," she muttered distractedly. Her fingers flew across the keys of her laptop. "Besides, I'm perfectly warm. Roy is in my lap and Beano is on my feet," she said, gifting Lex with an ironic smile. "As for heating me up fast, you know all you have to do is crook your little finger and I'm yours." She shook her head. "Masculine wiles. It's an appalling trick...but very heroic."

Lex chuckled. Whatever worked. He just wanted her. All the time. Couldn't get enough of her, and knew beyond a shadow of a doubt that he never would. He and Faith weren't into anything kinky, but he could understand the driving need for intimacy with the one you loved. Not just physical intimacy, either. There were other kinds. Sharing laughs, confessing fears, a touch of her hand, a certain telling glance. Those were the things he loved about being in love. And he couldn't have picked a better woman to fall in love with, a better partner to share his life with.

Word of Faith's successful *To Catch a Thief* party spread and he'd been booked practically every weekend since with similar events. He'd completed all the necessary renovations to the lodge—even a few that weren't necessary, but wanted—and he'd added an additional five employees to his staff. It gave Lex the time to do things he enjoyed, such as mingling with guests...and lingering in bed with his wife.

After a moment, she exited the file and lowered the screen. Then she nudged the dog from her lap and stood. "Okay, I'll come in now." She stared at the mountain. "It's just so pretty out here," she sighed. "The view is amazing."

Lex's gaze skimmed her gorgeous profile, and happiness and contentment—and desire, always desire—expanded in his chest. "That it is," he said softly.

She blushed adorably. "Thank you."

"I know a way you can thank me."

Her eyes twinkled and she gave a soft sigh. "I'll

just bet you do." She turned and started to the back door, then paused when he didn't readily follow. A sexy grin curled that lush, carnal mouth. "Come inside, badass, and tell me all about it."

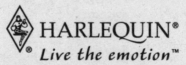

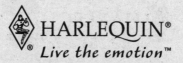

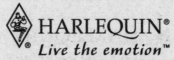